AT
WAR
WITH
EARL
PIERCE

By Ryan Fletcher

A
Four Eight One Designs
publication

"A person is a fool to become a writer. His only compensation is absolute freedom."

— Roald Dahl

Chapter 1

The room was filled with a thick haze of marijuana smoke and the sounds of laughter, heavy metal music, boisterous talking and clinking bottles and glasses.

"Leary you nutter, are you gonna have another rip of this billy?" a tall lanky tattooed skater with stretchers in his ears yelled out the back door of his business.

"Nah mate but I'll highjack another couple shots of whisky off you though," yelled a brown haired, blue eyed, average build, white male by the name of Lucas Leary, who was urinating on a corrugated iron fence at the back of the yard whilst whistling 'Highway To Hell' by AC/DC.

Lucas was a twenty-four year old itinerant worker who had grown-up in a small rural town in North Western Victoria. He was currently residing in a rented room above an old rustic pub on the border in Swan Hill and was dedicating his free time to writing articles and essays for a self-improvement magazine called 'Rek-Wiz-It', which was run by a Buddhist chiropractor named Vincent Tynan who lived in Ivanhoe.

Lucas was in the process of spending the night sipping
Gentleman Jack whisky and smoking joints at a local skater
shop hangout, where a billiard table and bar was set-up out
back. Caleb, the owner of the business, had invited Lucas
and the lads over to celebrate the New Year and the festivities
were going late into the night.

A consummate social butterfly, Lucas had met Caleb and
most of the lads in attendance whilst working a cash in hand
job at a local sign maker shop, which he'd been working
at for about nine months or so. Having finished up at the
shop that day to relocate, Lucas was spending the night
saying his farewells in an enticing atmosphere of music and
drunkenness.

"Fellas it's been a pleasure! Will likely be seeing you lot
down the track," Lucas announced to the partygoers as he
grabbed his colts filtered vanilla cigars.

Scattered shout-outs of farewell trailed Lucas' remarks as
Caleb escorted Lucas out to the front veranda.

"Mate if you are ever back this way look me up and I'll sort
you out with some cash in hand gigs," Caleb said to Lucas.

"Will do mate! Cheers on the night, had a bloody brilliant
time!" Lucas replied.

After making it back to his room at the pub and sleeping
for roughly seven hours, Lucas was spending the morning
sobering up, as he was due at his sister's place in Barooga
that evening. After washing up in the shared bathroom at the
end of the corridor, Lucas had popped into a bakery to grab a
spot of breakfast on his way to the bus station.

On his way through the township Lucas came across a small group of political organisers manning a booth handing out copies of a newspaper called 'The Neo National'.

The paper was produced by a political party called the National Electoral Committee (NEC). It had originally been formed as a political vehicle for the Australian Union of Liberties (AUOL), a pro-monarchist social credit anti-system organisation which had been holding seminars and lectures around the country since the mid 1940s.

The NEC had been infiltrated by acolytes of the American economist, political theoretician and perennial candidate Franklin Jones shortly after the party's formation. His supporters were zealously opposed to the British monarchy, predatory financiers, monetarism, drugs, war, as well as supporting the establishment of an Australian republic, national bank, large-scale infrastructure projects, space colonisation and the permeation of high class culture to the masses.

Lucas, who'd seen them periodically deployed at townships along the Murray River whilst working as a fruit picker, likened them to a clean cut version of the scruffy Socialist Association mob in Melbourne soliciting newspapers like 'Deport Whitey' or 'Black Left Monthly'.

"Sir have you heard about the parasitic looting being committed by the Leibler family?" asked an activist named Jim who was in his early twenties dressed in a grey short sleeved shirt.

"Can't say that I have. Who are the Leibler family?" Lucas

inquired.

"They are global system criminals weaponising drugs, pornography and speech suppression to deconstruct and destabilise Australian civilisation," Jim replied.

Intrigued by the rhetoric of the NEC activist, and stuck with the lengthy trip to his sister's place and nothing to read, Lucas grabbed a copy of 'The Neo National' and purchased two issues of a magazine published by the party called the Supervisory Intelligence Journal (SIJ).

One of the organisers, a young slender woman with dark curly hair named Vanessa, managed to get hold of Lucas' mobile number and offered to show him around the party headquarters in Coburg next time he was visiting the city.

"If you'd like to join us in the fight to rebuild Australia Lucas please don't hesitate to give us a call!" Vanessa affably invited.

"Thanks Vanessa, I'll definitely give it some thought!" Lucas sincerely replied.

Lucas pried himself away from the interaction with the Franklin Jones followers and continued to make his way to the bus station. As he arrived, loaded his bags and boarded the coach with his laptop and reading materials he proceeded to take a window seat midway up the aisle.

As the bus took off Lucas took a swig of his bottle of Pepsi and cracked open an issue of SIJ. Over the next couple of hours Lucas engrossed himself in well written essays espousing narratives about impending economic crisis, Green fascism, global depopulation, mass drugging, psychiatric experiments resulting in Manchurian candidate spree shooters, encroaching thermonuclear war, all of which was being instigated by the British crown and its operatives embedded in positions of power around the globe.

Whilst not fully convinced by the publications he was reading at face value, Lucas noted the appeal of the content by how it presented itself with a sense of crushing certainty.

As his bus pulled in to Cobram station, Lucas grabbed his belongings and waited on the roadside for his sister Sandra to pick him up. Sandra worked as a nurse at the hospital. Her husband Jason worked as a labourer around the region and their twin daughters, Lauren and Rachel, were just starting off kindergarten.

Lucas hadn't seen his sister since the last family gathering at Christmas the prior year and was looking forward to catching up with them. About ten minutes went by before Sandra pulled up alongside her brother in the family car.

"Hey bro how was your trip?" Sandra asked.

"Not bad sis," Lucas replied.

Sandra had the girls buckled up in their car seats behind them. Lucas turned around to hold their hands and say hello.

"How long you staying?" Sandra asked.

"Probably only for a couple of days, I have work lined up in the city," Lucas replied.

As Sandra drove the car Lucas looked down at his copy of
'The Neo National' and reflected on the proposal posed by
Vanessa, the organiser who'd offered to show him around the
Coburg based headquarters of the NEC. What could it hurt
to peek behind the curtain to see how their operation worked
firsthand?

It was about 6:30pm when they arrived at Sandra's place.
Jason had bought pizzas for dinner and Lucas was tired and
hungry. He managed to knock off half an entire large pizza
by himself before retiring to the guest room.

The next day Sandra had a day off work and invited Lucas
out to breakfast at Sweet Ness cafe. Lucas, Sandra and the
girls trekked on over and grabbed a table. Lucas ordered a
big breakfast of bacon, poached eggs, sausages, hash browns,
button mushrooms and grilled tomatoes with a side of coffee.

Lucas and Sandra were chatting about family escapades
when Lucas presented Sandra with his copy of 'The Neo
National'.

"Have you seen this before, sis?" Lucas asked.

Sandra looked the newspaper over and chuckled.

"No, I can't say that I have. Is this the new obsession you're
chasing, bro?" Sandra said.

Sandra was referencing a long history of eccentric
fascinations that had formed Lucas' passions over the years.
In primary school he'd been enthralled with paranormal
phenomena and UFOs, going so far as to say to family,
friends and teachers that he would go on to work at the

Search for Alien Intelligence (SEAI) Institute.

In high school, whilst perusing the Birthright Book Shop in Russell Street in Melbourne on holidays, Lucas had been introduced to the works of Klaus Fromm, a revisionist publisher and media producer living in Canada, who had produced content intertwining UFOs with secret weapons developed by the Nazis in Antarctica.

It was after high school that Lucas had dabbled with Freemasonry, Mormonism and Buddhism, the last of which is where Lucas had met Vincent who was the editor of Rek-Wiz-It magazine.

"I'm thinking about looking them up when I go down for the new job soon," Lucas said.

Sandra rolled her eyes and put her hand on Lucas' shoulder.

"Remember bro, if it sounds too good to be true it usually is. You should focus on getting a qualification and setting yourself up with a grounded profession and a wife instead of gallivanting around the country chasing odd jobs," Sandra said.

"What these guys are soliciting seems to have both a healthy dose of bad news with a side of solution, sis," Lucas said with a smile as he drank the rest of his coffee.

After breakfast Lucas, Sandra and the girls drove into Cobram to do some shopping and go to the library so Lauren and Rachel could borrow some children's books and Lucas could access the public Wi-Fi with his laptop (which he'd brought along with him).

Lucas began to analyse the NEC with some investigations via various search engines. Despite the NEC's fixation with the "British Empire of Monetarism" and characterising its political opponents as unironic "Nazis" and "Fascists", Lucas was surprised to find that the primary voice of hostility to their party came directly and indirectly from The Australia System Affairs Council (ASAC), the Executive Council of Australian Systemisation (ECAS), the Anti-Libel Alliance (ALA), the System Federation of Australia (SFA) and the Australian Human Rights Commission (AHRC).

Activist groups that utilised the facilities at Trades Hall, whom NEC organisers derided as "drug-crazed hippy lemmings running the MK-ULTRA maze of misdirection and murder", in turn denounced Franklin Jones supporters as "crypto-fascist cultists".

Likewise the establishment neo-conservatives and neo-liberals mocked the NEC as "kooks" and "conspiracy theorists".

Lucas was beginning to like the Franklin Jones supporters for the very reason they were detested by the system that had sooner bailed out billionaire corporate vampires than the average citizen working paycheque to paycheque. A system that had sent Australian citizens to die in geopolitical wars that had served system interests to the detriment of Australian interests. A system that had invested fool heartedly in intermittent "renewable" energy sources whilst outlawing a baseload power source that emitted zero greenhouse emissions during operation (i.e. nuclear energy and fusion energy).

That afternoon Lucas gave the NEC national hotline a call.
He conveyed to the staffer who answered that he'd run into
some of their organisers the day before and wished to take
Vanessa up on her offer of seeing the party's head office.
Lucas confirmed a date with the staffer in five days time, the
staffer conveying to Lucas that he'd relay the message to
Vanessa.

In the evening Lucas and Sandra went to see a movie at the
Cobram cinemas whilst Jason and the girls stayed home.
After the movie the two of them went to have coffee and cake
before calling it a night. Around 1:45pm the next day Lucas
said his farewells to Sandra and the family and caught the
2:45pm bus to Melbourne via Shepparton.

Vincent had offered Lucas the use of the granny flat at the
back of his house in Ivanhoe whilst he was working in the
city, which Lucas had gratefully accepted. After a restful
night of sleep, the next morning Lucas took to the city where
he started his first week cleaning high-rise windows.

At the end of the week Lucas made his way out to Coburg
to check out the NEC headquarters. Vanessa met Lucas out
front of the building and led him into an undercover gated
car-park. Leading Lucas up a staircase to a metal coded
locked door, the two of them entered the head office.

On entering Lucas noted an in-house printing press to the left
of him which clearly was used to produce the newspapers
and magazines disseminated by the organisers he'd met.
In front of him was a library of books spanning classic
literature, music, science and technology. To the left was
a meeting room, desks reserved for politicking and high-
pressure telephone sales, which led off to a neat kitchen area.

The atmosphere of the room exuded purpose and diligence. Vanessa guided Lucas over to the library area and proceeded to give him an overview of the campaigns they were currently working on with regards to party business, as well as articulating how the genius of Johannes Kepler, Carl Gauss, Bernhard Riemann and Gottfried Leibniz guided their organising.

Vanessa further outlined that Isaac Newton was a tactical fiction of the British empire tantamount to "Pagan worship", that Charles Darwin was a "fraud", and that Sheldon Soros was a "British agent" hell-bent on destroying the Equal Party (the party of which Franklin Jones sought the nomination for President of the United States seven times since 1980).

Lucas was hardly taken back by the views espoused by Vanessa. Over the last couple of years Lucas had experienced firsthand the opinions of blue haired feminists flocking to the ranks of the National Labour Students Council. With said feminists espousing views about castrating all White male children at birth and have existing male adults guilty of "toxic masculinity" pay reparations to females for their role in amplifying "systemic patriarchal oppression" against girls and women, Lucas was far more receptive as to what Vanessa had to say.

"Can I get you a cuppa Lucas?" Vanessa asked.

"Sure. White coffee with one sugar thanks mate," Lucas replied.

As Vanessa went to the kitchen Lucas looked over some reading materials on a table next to the bookcase. Two publications, a book titled 'Drug Empire: Britain's War To Dope The World' and a report titled 'Manufacturing Murder in Australia: MKULTRA Conditioning Is System Psyop Suicide', immediately drew Lucas's attention.

The notion of an overarching global cabal organising the mass drugging of the population via the legal white markets, illegal black markets and everything in between, as said Cabal socially engineered the population with various psychiatric operations, was a proposition Lucas all too willingly believed to be true.

As Vanessa returned with the coffee she inquired in so many words as to whether Lucas was interested in joining the NEC, to which Lucas expressed interest. Vanessa presented Lucas with a membership form to fill out and encouraged him to purchase a copy of a book published by the party titled 'How Australia Will Survive The System Onslaught'.

Lucas paid the nominal dues and an extra twenty dollars for the book then told Vanessa he was due elsewhere. Lucas thanked Vanessa for having showed him the party's head office and proceeded to exit the building.

It was about 12:30pm by the time Lucas had caught a tram a short way down Sydney Road to The Brunswick Green pub and ordered himself a pint of beer. He found himself a table out in the beer garden and began to look through the book he'd acquired.

Whilst slowly knocking back four pints Lucas scrolled over the content encompassing economic recovery via a New Bretton Woods plan, the construction of high-speed rail routes connecting the Eurasian Land Bridge, and large scale irrigation projects designed to "green the deserts".

After about an hour later Lucas double backed to Mediterranean wholesalers, an Italian supermarket and coffee bar, to order himself another coffee with an added cannoli. As he contently sat there sipping away at his beverage and reflecting on the NEC milieu Lucas got an idea for an essay he could write for Rek-Wiz-It.

Borrowing the NEC's dichotomy between the British Empire versus the "American method", Lucas decided to write a story that would illustrate the two competing forces of light and dark, like Golding's 'Lord Of The Flies', Orwell's 'Animal Farm', or Commander Rockwell's 'Fable Of The Ducks And The Hens'.

Catching a tram to Ivanhoe and making his way back to Vincent's place; Lucas started to map out the plot for his tale.

Set in the year 2050 the forces loyal to the British crown had plunged the planet into an apocalyptic battleground where plagues were met with pharmaceutical, medical supplies and personal protective equipment (PPE) profits, 'mental health' resulted in domestication and enslavement, and breeding had become a total dysgenic inversion of "survival of the fittest".

Counter intentional dissidents dubbed "terrorists" by the trillioniare oligarchy were eradicated by private military companies who'd fully replaced national standing armies, as the world had ostensibly been reformed in a few short decades to a series of economic regions that replaced long standing nation states.

The culture directing mass society had devolved into such a

hellscape that only the billionaire and millionaire disciples of the trillioniare oligarchy were privy to the transcendent culture that caused them to replicate as ostensibly a separate species to the malnourished masses.

Weaponized "biodiversity" by the transnational climate cult had resulted in a broad sweeping "Malthusian catastrophe", which saw habitual famine and war engulf the four corners of the earth.

Only the "Loyal Organisers" were the exception to the rule. Ostensibly a guerrilla intelligentsia whom operated under the system's radar in order to liberate the masses from the trillioniare oligarchy's tyranny, the "Loyal Organisers" disseminated dissident publications and facilitated training camps on how to disrupt the demonic oligarchs.

As Lucas typed away at his laptop like a man possessed by a great epiphany, he drank down four cups of white coffee. By 11:00pm that night Lucas had finished writing his story, which he'd titled '2050: Revolt Against The Synarchist Vampires'. He promptly e-mailed it to Vincent for consideration in the next issue of Rek-Wiz-It.

The next morning after breakfast, Lucas decided to commute into the city to peruse Queen Victoria market and take in the city scene. By about 10:45am Lucas reached his destination and hunted for a bargain or two in the myriad of market stalls spruiking treasures to the avid consumer.

Apart from buying himself an Akubra hat and some new shirts, Lucas came across some reprints of a 1944 comic books titled 'The Legion of Space: An Interplanetary Adventure Strip' by Phillip Wearne. Initially attracted by the retro Flash Gordon style drawings, as well as the meagre price, Lucas began to recall the name Phillip Wearne having been raised by his grandfather Frank Leary, who had been a hardcore Labor man all his life.

In the 1950s Phillip Wearne, a former clerk for the Royal Australian Air Force, had headed a business called Australian Trade Union Press (ATUP).

ATUP became a highly profitable venture for Wearne when he began brokering deals with Union officials, who he'd met through the Australian Labor Party, to produce their various publications for free.

By selling advertising space in said publications to interested groups and businesses, whilst in turn capitalising off the purchasing power of the various Unions memberships, their collective consumer solidarity inevitably led to Wearne making sizeable sums with little effort.

Around 1958 Wearne got involved with Scientology. Like the New Religious Movement's founder L. Ron Hubbard, Wearne's prior service in the armed forces, flare for science fiction and shrewd sense for business made for a formidable force.

In four short years, after dabbling with the subject, Wearne parted with Scientology to initiate publishing projects of his own that borrowed concepts from Scientology. One such publication titled 'Probe', with an article titled 'Security Checking Made Easy' (1961), ended up leading to Wearne being targeted for surveillance by the Australian Security Intelligence Organisation (ASIO).

By 1970 Wearne was dead from an apparent methaqualome (aka Quaalude) overdose. According to Frank, who was not shy about expressing opinions about conspiratorial activities, Wearne had been assassinated by either an agent or agent of influence who were loyal to Tory plutocrats either domestic or foreign.

Ironically enough Lucas soon was to be following a similar path to Wearne's, filled with intrigue, espionage, frame-ups and assassinations.

Chapter 2

Lucas trekked from Queen Victoria Market to The Drunken Poet pub for a pint of Guinness and a sandwich. Whilst flipping through the comics he'd bought and nursing his pint, a twenty-six year old man named Jacob approached him and struck up a conversation.

"Hey mate, I see you're a Sci-Fi fan," Jacob said.

"Kind of," Lucas replied.

Jacob had fiery red hair and whiskers, green eyes and was of a slimmer build than Lucas. Jacob wore a Blade Runner t-shirt, denim jeans and black running shoes.

Lucas invited Jacob to sit with him and have a beer. As they chatted Lucas discovered that Jacob came from a wealthy family. His father was the largest supplier of umbrellas, waterproof ponchos and promotional sunglasses to various retailers and sporting entertainment events in the country.

Jacob, who preferred to present himself as a working class

punter, preferred to spend his time as an illustrator for various authors around the city and forge associations with protesters that hung around the New International Bookshop at Trades Hall. He also had connections with uppity wannabe gangsters who emulated The Carlton Crew.

Lucas had conveyed to Jacob about his current employment situation as he moonlighted as a writer. It was about 3:30pm when the two of them parted company but before they did, Jacob handed Lucas a business card.

"Just in case you need someone to sketch up some pictures for your writing projects mate," Jacob said.

"Cheers mate! I might just take you up on that," Lucas replied.

Lucas proceeded to make his way to the train at Flinders Street Station. By the time Lucas made it back to his accommodation in Ivanhoe, Vincent and his wife Larissa were getting ready to prepare dinner.

"Hey Lucas, I love the story you e-mailed me last night. I had a chance to read it this morning," Vincent said to Lucas as he came through the front door.

"Have dinner with Larissa and I so we can talk more about it."

"Sure, sounds great mate!" Lucas replied.

Over dinner Vincent outlined to Lucas his idea to serialise Lucas' story. By expanding '2050: Revolt Against The Synarchist Vampires' into a dozen volumes, Lucas could map out in broader detail how the 'Loyal Organisers' inflicted their enlightening blows against the trillionaire tyranny.

Vincent further suggested that Lucas publish the serialised work under a pseudonym. Lucas suggested the name 'Earl Pierce', which took the surname of Dr. William Luther Pierce (the author of "The Turner Diaries") and the first name from the novel's protagonist Earl Turner. Vincent liked the name and agreed that the next issue of Rek-Wiz-It, which was due to be published at the beginning of next month, would feature the first written instalment by the elusive writer 'Earl Pierce'.

The next morning Lucas made his way into the city to start another week's work cleaning high rise windows. Lucas liked the job as it paid well and wasn't overly stressful. The Akubra hat, which Lucas had bought from Queen Victoria Market, was ideal for protecting him from the sun as he abseiled down past lemmings working away in their stuffy corporate offices.

Lucas, who never lasted longer than eleven or twelve months in a job, figured he could keep pace with this gig for a good while. After a day's work Lucas would spend two hours knocking back a few beers with his work colleagues, then head out to Ivanhoe to either have dinner with Vincent and Larissa or a meal at the Ivanhoe Hotel.

In the late evenings Lucas would take to typing out the multifaceted instalments which outlined how the 'Revolt Against The Synarchist Vampires' would transpire.

By the time the next issue was ready to be sold at various outlets along the East Coast of Australia, Lucas had already completed two more volumes to add to the series. Over the next fortnight Vincent had received a healthy amount of fan mail regarding the contributions of 'Earl Pierce'.

Before the second instalment was to be published, Vincent and Lucas went for lunch in the city at Gopals restaurant which was one of Lucas' favourite places for a casual eating experience that catered to a Buddhist friendly diet.

"Lucas your story is going down better than expected! So far sales have doubled on this last issue," Vincent said.

"Cheers mate! Hopefully we start seeing those numbers quadruple," Lucas replied.

Lucas had been giving some thought over the last couple of weeks to the offer posed by his chance encounter with Jacob. During lunch Lucas proposed that Vincent assess Jacob's portfolio and see if he would be worth hiring as an illustrator for the future series. Vincent agreed to consider Jacob as a possible contributor on the project.

Later that week Jacob dropped by Vincent's office with two neatly presented art portfolios. Vincent was enamoured by the energetic expressiveness of Jacob's work which captured wild, weird, distorted, fanciful visions and an eclectic range of subject matter. Vincent determined Jacob was ideal to be Lucas' creative deputy.

It was a week and half out from the print date of the second volume when Jacob was officially contracted to produce some drawings for the next issue. Come publishing time Jacob had produced a series of twisted apocalyptic images that resembled a combination of sketches in the style of Brett Whiteley mixed with the artistic horror of Clive Barker.

Sales on the second issue saw a steady increase from the last, so much so that it began to garner attention from a certain newspaper commentator as "an up and coming serialised work of fiction generating a dangerous indulgence to a niche fandom around the country". The so called "niche fandom" which the commentator was alluding to was a part of the growing fervour across Australia that was seeking solidarity and determination against the establishment.

With the politicians persistently pushing policy in the direction of detriment against citizens, the media pretentiously lecturing said citizens of the importance of embracing every hyper-liberal freakish fad they could dream up, and the international money masters sabotaging the nation economically, commercially and industrially, it was needless to say that the market of support was ripe.

Before the third issue was due to be released Lucas received a call from Vanessa. She had invited him to attend an evening webcast meeting at the Coburg office on the weekend, which was to headline a speech and dialogue session with Franklin Jones from his "war room" in Leesburg, Virginia.

Lucas was hardly inexperienced when it came to political meetings. Having attended various functions around the state since the age of thirteen, ranging from the so-called "moon bat left" to the "lunar right", it had become a sort of perverse past-time for him throughout his teen years whilst intermittently partying with school mates at local drinking sessions.

Not one to say no to such an offer Lucas accepted Vanessa's invitation. After finishing out the work week Lucas

commuted to Coburg by tram to attend the webcast meeting.
In attendance were a bunch of small farmers, business
owners, former councillors (from the city to the bush), a
corporate water management board member, student age
activist types, some frontline union representatives and
various people that had seemingly struck a chord with the
party's propaganda.

It was not a complex notion for Lucas that amongst those
congregated at the meeting were spies working for various
private acronym agencies with loyalties to the Anti-Libel
Alliance (ALA), that included direct agents working for
ASIO officers.

As the meeting kicked off Franklin Jones was provided
an introduction by one of his close confidants Jessica
Freeman, who had been involved with the international
movement since the 1970s. When Franklin Jones took the
podium he began to outline how the "malicious Green
fascists" were strategically seeking to operate the thirty odd
seawater desalination plants around Australia on "genocidal
intermittent 'renewable' energy sources".

He proceeded to outline how Fusion energy not only
addressed the issue of baseload power but that it would be
extremely cost efficient for the foreseeable future of Australia
when contrasted with said renewable energy sources and
even nuclear power. Franklin Jones spoke for hours about
a myriad of topics ranging from economy, engineering,
infrastructure development, society, culture, farming and so
on.

After the webcast had finished attendees conversed around
the office. Lucas struck up a conversation with a bloke

named Geoff who owned a bike emporium and a lady named Amanda who ran an alternative medicine practice with twelve qualified medical practitioners and a store selling health products, natural goods and supplements.

"Hey cobber, whereabouts you hail from?" Geoff asked Lucas.

"Originally from Robinvale but have been moving around a bit over the last couple of years. How about yourself, Geoff?" Lucas asked.

"The family and I live in Melbourne but we have property up in Benalla," Geoff replied.

"Are you working at the moment, Lucas?" Amanda asked.

"Yeah, currently working off the side of skyscrapers cleaning windows," Lucas replied.

As the three chatted back and forth Lucas ascertained that Geoff and Amanda had also grown up in rural based working class families similar to his own. Geoff, who had been a zealous supporter of B. A. Santamaria and the Democratic Labor Party, had been virulently opposed to the Australian communists since he was a kid. Amanda, who'd been a card carrying Union member who'd been involved with the Populist Patriots Party (PPP), had too been hostile to the 'New Left'.

Geoff and Amanda gave their phone numbers to Lucas and invited him to keep in touch.

As folks started leaving for the night Lucas proceeded to

once again catch a tram down Sydney road to The Brunswick Green pub and order himself a pint of beer. Striking up a conversation with some musicians and barflies, Lucas enjoyed a couple of hours drinking Carlton Draught and smoking Colts filtered vanilla cigars whilst listening to the live Jazz music.

It was late when Lucas got back to his accommodation in Ivanhoe. Jacob had e-mailed Lucas and Vincent copies of the drawings for the latest edition of 'Revolt Against The Synarchist Vampires' and Vincent had replied by writing approvingly "top job fellas".

The next morning Lucas commuted into the city to peruse the Theosophical Society's library and bookshop at 124-130 Russell Street, spending a couple hours looking through the esoteric books ranging from Anthroposophy, Kabbalah and Thelema occultism. He then took a short walk across the road to look through the Birthright Book Shop, which had titles from C. H. Douglas, David Irving, Carleton Putnam, Gary Allen and Henry A. Clark.

Lucas, who would often take to analysing subjects on the periphery of public awareness, would channel what he read into palatable works that allegorically illustrated abstract concepts of truth. One might observantly say Lucas believed in the proverb of catching more flies with honey than with vinegar.

Around 1:00pm Lucas met with Jacob at The Elephant and Wheelbarrow pub in Bourke Street for lunch, where the two talked about the trajectory of 'Revolt Against The Synarchist Vampires'. Lucas alluded to Jacob in so many words that he hoped his serialised story would help disrupt the establishment's electrified drug induced hypnosis over the public.

Jacob was someone who would be the most avid of adherents if he thought it to be something he could get in on the ground floor with. It was obvious that Lucas and Jacob's personality types complimented their synchronising skill set and business partnership.

After lunch Lucas and Jacob grabbed a coffee and parted ways for the afternoon. Lucas grabbed a train back out to Ivanhoe to catch up with Vincent. When Lucas arrived, Vincent was having a chuckle about some letters to the editor he'd received.

"Lucas mate, you are starting to get your share of hate mail coming in now!" Vincent exclaimed with a smile.

"Oh yeah? How butthurt are the critics mate?" Lucas enquired.

"Listen to this... Dear Editor, Your latest serialised fiction work '2050: Revolt Against The Synarchist Vampires' is clearly a fascist diatribe using crypto racist canards to cloak you true intentions. I recommend that everyone who supports love, inclusion, diversity and democracy lodges complaints with the Australian Human Rights Commission (AHRC) and the Anti-Libel Alliance (ALA) so as to have Rek-Wiz-It magazine shutdown for sedition against multicultural Australia! Sincerely, Talia" Vincent read aloud.

"Are you going to publish it in the Letters to the Editor section in the next issue?" Lucas asked in jest.

"You better believe it mate! 'Revolt Against The Synarchist Vampires' is starting to reveal the sort of anti free-speech bloodsuckers we're up against," Vincent replied.

Vincent had a particular pet hatred for these sorts of agitators. Rek-Wiz-It, similar to Australian publications like Nexus and New Dawn, would regularly be maligned as "conspiracy theorist" and "militia magazines" by establishment collaborators seeking to sanitize the public discourse.

"We're going to send a clear message to this mob mate that Rek-Wiz-It will not kowtow to their demands for censorship!" Vincent sternly stated.

It was the release day of the third instalment of 'Revolt Against The Synarchist Vampires' and Vincent could already sense a further increase in nationwide sales of the issue. With unofficial fan pages beginning to pop up on social media, Vincent had the idea of starting a formal fandom domain via the Rek-Wiz-It website where people could fluidly provide feedback to himself, Lucas and Jacob.

Taking to Va Tutto Restaurant for lunch to celebrate part three of the serial Lucas, Vincent and Jacob were cheerily enjoying their meals with wine and beer when Larissa rang. She conveyed to Vincent that state counter-terrorism officers had shown up on their doorstep.

Apparently the two attending officers were seeking to "chat" with Vincent about the author of 'Revolt Against The Synarchist Vampires'. As the front and back wire doors were readily kept locked at the household, Larissa had told the attending officers to leave, but not before one officer left a business card between the wire door and the door frame.

Vincent, who was hardly perturbed by what Larissa had relayed to him, simply reassured her that "There's nothing to worry about, hun. I'll speak to Mark about it." Mark Jameson was a solicitor Vincent used for various legal advices but mostly pertaining to his assorted businesses.

"Hey lads, it looks like the state police intelligence unit are wanting to know more about our mate 'Earl Pierce'!" Vincent scoffed.

"Does it sound like they know more than they're letting on?" Lucas asked.

"Not sure. I suspect they're phishing for the moment," Vincent replied.

"On the off chance that they might know more than they're letting on mate I know a place close to the train station in Broadmeadows you can bunker down in," Jacob said.

"Cheers mate! I might have to take you up on that offer. When is the accommodation available?" Lucas enquired.

"Right away if need be mate," Jacob replied.

After the three finished lunch and drove back to Vincent's place, Lucas gathered together his laptop and other belongings for a subtle getaway out to Broadmeadows. On the off chance that 'Earl Pierce' was to be dubbed a subversive operative by the Joint Counter Terrorism Team (JCTT), Lucas thought it important that Vincent and Larissa were seen not to be harbouring a dissident writer at their home.

Jacob accompanied Lucas on the half hour journey by public transport to Broadmeadows train station. A short walk from the adjacent Anglicare Broadmeadows offices was a small two bedroom house that Jacob's uncle owned, which Jacob sporadically used as a place to stay when not at his parents place in Carlton.

"I've let my uncle know that you'll be staying here. If you want to stay a while just kick up $350 per week and I'll cover you on the bond," Jacob said.

"Cheers mate, can do," Lucas replied.

As Vincent and Lucas already relied on end-to-end encrypted email services to communicate when writing content remotely, Lucas was somewhat less worried about communications pinpointing his location if he needed to take off in a hurry. Regularly using public Wi-Fi hotspots, Lucas would be able to send new instalments of 'Revolt Against The Synarchist Vampires' to Vincent with ostensible peace of mind.

Lucas had already invested a healthy amount of money into cryptocurrencies like Bitcoin and was astute at keeping off the radar if need be. However with a lingering hint of paranoia about police snooping around Vincent's place, Lucas felt more secure if he was out of the state, even though he knew that ASIO would be coordinating with neighbouring state and territory police units if things escalated.

Spending the afternoon sipping coffee at a McDonald's Restaurant in Broadmeadows whilst scouting out jobs and accommodation in New South Wales (NSW) Lucas began to strategise his next move forward.

Although his sister Sandra and brother Jack both lived in NSW, and his other sister Elise lived in South Australia, Lucas thought it safer not to make the issues of 'Earl Pierce' an interstate family affair as it were. His parents Jacinta and Scott were definitely not an ideal place to stay as they lived in Ballarat, Victoria.

Lucas, who had NSW contacts from Wodonga to Byron Bay, made a list from his contacts notebook to call over the next fortnight as he finished up working in the city. Having lasted over four months working as a high rise window cleaner, as he penned a serialised work of fiction that invoked "politically motivated violence", Lucas was once again relocating.

Chapter 3

It was the period between Michael Trumble being the first
Australian Prime Minister to attend the Sydney Gay and
Lesbian Mardi Gras and the first Australian Prime Minister
to be virally streamed circle dancing at a Sydney house of
worship (which was receiving sizeable tax-payer subsidies
for armed security).

Daniel Drumpf had just officially been nominated as the
Republican presidential candidate at the Republican National
Convention. Meanwhile Lucas was taking a walk along an
oceanfront pathway in Coffs Harbour, taking in the serene
sea view and clean cool air as he reflected on the direction of
his writing.

He had secured two jobs working alternating shifts between
a pizza parlour and a fish and chip shop, both which were
paying him cash in hand off the books, hence not notifying
the Australian Tax Office (ATO) of his whereabouts.

Though his income was meagre his rent was ostensibly non-
existent, as he was bunkering down in a cabin at the back

of a property owned by a family friend named John. John, who had worked as an engineer in the mines in Kalgoorlie, had decided to set himself up on the East Coast working maintenance jobs around the region whilst he wrote his great Australian novel.

The most John expected of Lucas was to fork out some dough to buy them a slab of beer to share every now and then.

Lucas had just finished writing volume nine of 'Revolt Against The Synarchist Vampires' and Vincent had overseen the production of volume seven. Rek-Wiz-It magazine was being inundated with correspondence expressing both zealous support and seething hatred.

Citing the Racial Discrimination Act 1975 and the use of "allegorical racist canards" the Australian Human Rights Commission (AHRC) and Anti-Libel Alliance (ALA) had lodged frivolous cease and desist letters against Rek-Wiz-It magazine.

However Vincent was countering these cease and desist letters from the AHRC and the ALA with his own cease and desist letters after the news services of these organisations were characterising Rek-Wiz-It magazine as the "Australian Der Stürmer".

Meanwhile an article published in the Sydney Afternoon Messenger and The Epoch newspapers titled 'Who Is 'Earl Pierce'? The Far Right Hater Destroying Our Democracy" had reinforced the scapegoating of the Herald Star which denounced the elusive 'Earl Pierce' as "an anti-democratic Leftist subversive".

The publicity from this finger wagging by the establishment press was helping to amplify the sales of Rek-Wiz-It magazine, so much so that copies were selling out in most stores where it was available for purchase.

Jacob, who had ostensibly been cast out from his social circles around Trades Hall for being a "fascist ally", was eager for a change of scenery away from the inner city sideshow of communist intersectional politics. He relocated to Mildura and set up an art studio out the back of a rented flat whilst bartending on the side.

Jacob had struck up a close relationship with an eighteen year old young woman named Emily who had brown hair, blue eyes, a unicursal hexagram tattooed on her left upper thigh and a Black Sun symbol tattooed on her right upper thigh.

The two had met when Jacob had sought the services of Emily for a tarot card reading in deriving guidance over the future of his creative works. Emily, an autodidact artist herself who worked in the food services industry as a waitress, moonlighted as a psychic whom sketched and painted surrealist artworks portraying visions of 'root races' hailing from Hyperborea, Lemuria, and Atlantis.

Whilst Jacob and Emily shared an interest in science fiction and art, they more importantly were attracted to the ideas of the occult and revolutionary futurism. This shared belief is what gravitated Emily into the orbit of Rek-Wiz-It as a visual media contributor.

Meanwhile Lucas had taken to attending various different church services in the Coffs Harbour area and was beginning to warm up to The Church of Jesus Christ of Latter-Day Saints (LDS), which had an aesthetic and organisational structure that rekindled Lucas' past experience with Freemasonry.

The LDS church, whose American roots had a rich history of defiance against non-LDS government authority, attracted a congregation of clean cut devotees that abstained from vices and worked the equivalent of a second or third job on church projects. Church members (i.e. Mormons) were kept within a holistic milieu control consisting of LDS produced magazines, books, videos, music, films, blogs and other assorted digital media.

Even though Lucas was hardly someone free from socially abstaining from vices like alcohol, tobacco or coffee he quickly discovered a particular kinship with one of the members of the congregation.

Joseph was a blonde haired, blue eyed, thirty-four year old White male who enjoyed firearms, fishing and boating. He owned a number of bolt action rifles and shotguns and his father Graham owned a Pacific Sea Craft 34 cruising yacht.

An avid fan of science fiction novellas and sporadic reader of various conservative magazines like The Spectator and Quadrant, Joseph was a dedicated subscriber to Rek-Wiz-It. Following the ongoing exploits of the "Loyal Organizers" as the saga of 'Revolt Against The Synarchist Vampires' unfolded, Joseph's abiding connection with the serialised story was akin to his religious conviction of the golden plates at the core of the LDS faith.

Spending time hanging out around Eric & Deb's Homemade

Ice Cream parlour sipping milkshakes as they trekked along the jetty and marina walkway, Lucas and Joseph would regularly converse about politics, religion and topics that would be deemed in the normal sphere of discourse to be "conspiracy theorist" in nature.

Joseph ascribed to the worldview that a coterie of wealthy liberal plutocrats were seeking to socially engineer the world into a dysgenic dystopian society suppressed by a tyrannical state that over regulated citizens' lives whilst simultaneously being unwilling to enforce fundamental protective laws.

Politically Joseph was a conscientious objector when it came to voting. He believed anyone worth voting for was ostensibly rigged to lose by the ruling elite, and that ballots were about as legitimate as toilet paper under the current corrupt system. He abstained from getting vaccinated and believed abortion was tantamount to murder.

It was Joseph's profound distrust of the system that caused Lucas to confide in Joseph one morning whilst walking along the oceanfront as they nursed blue heaven milkshakes.

"Joseph mate I've been writing for Rek-Wiz-It magazine for awhile now but I recently got the revelation to start publishing under a pseudonym after a chance meeting with the National Electoral Committee." Lucas said.

"Sounds like divine intervention brother! What's the pseudonym you're running with?" Joseph asked.

"Earl Pierce," Lucas replied.

"Brother I love your 'Revolt Against The Synarchist

Vampires' serialisation! It is pure gold! From what I've been witnessing it's been getting under the skin of all the right people!" Joseph exclaimed.

"Cheers mate, I appreciate it! We just need to keep the pseudonym on the down low. We've had some interest from the state intelligence units come after us over it," Lucas said.

"Of course brother, you can rely on me! Would you be able to put in a good word to your editor for me?" Joseph eagerly asked.

"Sure mate! Are you interested in contributing to the magazine?" Lucas inquired.

"Absolutely! I have some inspired writings that I think would add to the high standard of Rek-Wiz-It!" Joseph wholeheartedly stated.

Joseph would soon begin publishing his work under the pseudonym 'Hyrum Young', a composite of the LDS church leaders Hyrum Smith and Brigham Young. His first article titled 'A White Delightsome Blood Atonement' would soon be called an "ostensible white supremacist Fatwa" by ASIO.

Vincent was currently in full swing publishing a trove of articles written by people caught up in the populist craze of Daniel Drumpf's candidacy for President. The U.S. Presidential election date on November 8th was only four short months away, and activist collectives in the metropolitan areas were mobilising against "institutional White Supremacy".

With hyper-liberalism having accelerated over the last couple years there was a bourgeoning base of Paleoconservative, Hoppean Libertarian, Fascist, White Nationalist, anti-feminist, anti-democracy and anti-system sentiment flaring up in the online noosphere.

The Australian national media, who had been working in tandem with the corporate propaganda cartels in America to circulate Central Intelligence Agency (CIA) press kits, were working overtime to present Daniel Drumpf as a "white supremacist" spearheading the influence of the "far right" into the American government.

In actuality the encroaching Drumpf presidency was soon to install one of the most gaudy and virulent expressions of the system into the White House, which in turn would oversee the most extensive international crackdowns against white dissidents by the "Five Eyes" Anglosphere intelligence alliance compromised of Australia, Canada, New Zealand, the United Kingdom, and the United States.

Agencies like ASIO, who had a priority status on Islamic terrorism following the 2001 September 11 attacks on the World Trade Center and Pentagon, and 2002 Bali bombings in the tourist district of Kuta in Bali, were incorporating "white supremacists" into their focus. The risk of an association forming between Islamists and white nationalists was internally termed a "two pronged threat against the system" by ASIO.

By the time volume eight of 'Revolt Against The Synarchist Vampires' had made it into stores Rek-Wiz-It magazine had become the most visible and primary periodical for 'far-right' content in Australia. ASIO, who fluidly made risk assessments of groups based on a mitigated threat level if said group was 'reformist rather than revolutionary', deemed the growing influence of Rek-Wiz-It magazine to be highly problematic.

Rek-Wit-It, which had a large committed consumer base that wasn't bound to subscription lists, had the potential of being a propaganda source that would cater to lone wolves or radicalised 'cell groups' in carrying out 'politically motivated violence'.

ASIO were reluctant to shut-down Rek-Wiz-It as a subversive entity at this stage, as they only had conjecture from 'experts' lacking in credulity to offer up to the public. With virtually no documented activities alluding to an actual terrorist threat, the best ASIO could portray Rek-Wiz-It magazine as was a publication disseminating content that "potentially could undermine the authority of the Government of Australia".

Also ASIO determined it to be counter-productive to directly proceed heavy handed against Rek-Wiz-It at this stage, as the magazine was helping to galvanise certain 'agent in place' controlled opposition factions that were fermenting the surge in support for Daniel Drumpf's candidacy for the White House.

However indirect ASIO funding was provided to Trades Hall tacticians, who coordinated black bloc anarchist street thug cadres, to produce counterpropaganda against Vincent and his colleagues. By framing the speech in Rek-Wiz-It magazine as "violence" and justifying the violence of said anarchist cadres as "speech", ASIO were able to manufacture a covert agency induced antithesis which could be used to mobilise malleable malcontents against the 'far right'.

Vincent wrote in an e-mail to Lucas and Jacob:

> *G'day fellas,*
>
> *It has come to my attention that the gay ops being stoked by our counter-terrorism buddies are quickly accelerating. Might I suggest we all start making arrangements for a swift retreat off-the-grid and/or outside of Australia if circumstances shift against us?*
>
> *Regards,*
> *V*

By the end of September, with volume nine of 'Revolt Against The Synarchist Vampires' having been published, Vincent had organised a fortnight holiday away from his chiropractor practice and was keen to catch up with Lucas and Jacob. The three lads decided to meet at a midpoint between where each were currently residing, deciding on the regional city of Bathurst in NSW.

Lucas and Joseph travelled down in Joseph's Ford Falcon Ute, Jacob and Emily travelled over via Emily's White Kia Rio, and Vincent and Larissa travelled up in their Ford Ranger. The six of them arrived on Friday 23rd September, checking into the Panorama Motel and proceeding to go out for dinner at the Church Bar Woodfired Pizza restaurant on Ribbon Gang Lane.

Over cocktails and beers the six of them discussed the impending probability of a Drumpf presidency and the trajectory of Rek-Wiz-It magazine under such a presidency.

"I think the prospect of a Drumpf administration will only help amplify the various White dissident factions that have been cheering him on along the campaign trail," Jacob said.

"I'm not fully convinced about him. Need to keep in mind that the golden gangster ally is the protégé of homo system blackmailer Roy Priest," Emily warned.

"Too right, I trust tranny loving Drumpf about as much as I trust a degree from Drumpf university!" Larissa agreed.

"It doesn't matter which one of the two candidates win out of the red and blue cartels, the CIA will have them owned dead to rights by either money, ideology, compromise, or ego. Best we can do is channel the manufactured aura around Drumpf to our advantage," Lucas interjected.

"True. If life serves you up a turd sandwich or a giant douche you need to highlight that its system certified and that you oppose being taxed for it in order to sponsor state terrorism," Vincent affirmed.

It was safe to say that everyone in attendance had a healthy amount of scepticism about Drumpf being a sincere candidate. However there was an undeniable surge in white voter support for him mixed with the glaring dreadfulness of Drumpf's opponent that led them to conclude continued support for Drumpf was the best strategy for Rek-Wiz-It.

After a night of getting drunk on alcohol, politics and publishing the next morning the six of them visited the former home of Labor Prime Minister Ben Chifley, which had been converted into a museum and education centre dedicated to his legacy. The house was an aesthetic step back into the golden age of 1940s White Australia, which showcased an eclectic range of household furnishings, kitchenware and personal effects that pre-dated the depression era.

Ironically is was under the Chifley administration that ASIO had been created.

Between seeing the sights and grabbing coffee and cake at the various cafes whilst perusing the local art galleries, Lucas, Vincent and Jacob discussed contingency plans for publishing 'Revolt Against The Synarchist Vampires' in case legal pressures disrupted the publication of Rek-Wiz-It magazine.

"I've spoken with a number of hardcopy and digital publications fellas and have managed to organize a dozen or so to syndicate the previous and future volumes of Lucas' story," Vincent said.

"How best to get written and artwork copy to them mate?" Lucas asked Vincent.

"Preferably via encrypted e-mails as we've been doing. So you are not having to rely on me as a middleman I've made you lads a list of e-mail contacts to forward content on to," Vincent replied.

"Looks like the intel goon squad will be playing a game of whack-a-mole with us," Jacob stated.

"True!" Lucas and Vincent chimed in together.

On the Monday Vincent, Larissa, Jacob and Emily travelled to Cowra to venture through the Japanese Garden and cultural centre, spending a night at the Townhouse Motel, whilst Lucas and Joseph made their way back up the coast to Coffs Harbour.

During the next week, as volume ten of 'Revolt Against The Synarchist Vampires' was being prepped and published, Lucas watched closely as the provocative dirty tricks that had been a signature characteristic of the Presidential campaign began to vamp up into overdrive.

Dedicated activists, campaigners, firebrands and trolls who'd flooded social media with memes and messages bolstering what Ivy League CIA assets had termed "weaponized irony", was being doubled down on by all involved.

Artwork that Jacob had created for 'Revolt Against The Synarchist Vampires' was being widely disseminated in both original form and also with varying visual edits to imply a particular counter establishment message.

Though Drumpf had predominately honed in on anti-Islamic rhetoric throughout the campaign, it was the system operatives who were seemingly playing up the jitters the most. Even despite Drumpf having explicitly denounced "anti-systemists", organisations like the Anti-Libel Alliance (ALA) were still arm flailing about the "spectre of white supremacy" under a Drumpf administration.

A dozen or so hate crime hoaxes, such as misshapen anti-system symbols being scrawled on system homes, cemetery headstones and houses of worship across America had been determined by law enforcement to have been carried out by sycophantic pro-system students. Naturally this was quickly whitewashed away by the mainstream media.

Whilst these low level failed frame-ups were largely transparent to the average citizen, it was myriad of government false flag operations that were largely concealed, as if like an iceberg hidden by seawater.

The Drumpf ship, which was riding a zealous wave of white voter support into the White House, would soon be crashing into a deliberate distraction that would cause said ship to dump out a load of oily blackness into the surrounding proverbial waters.

Chapter 4

It was a cool cloudy day around noon on Tuesday 1st November, 2016 in Melbourne. Light rain was beginning to fall down upon the Victorian capital and an atmosphere of liveliness exuded the central business district.

Dr. Jonathan Foxman, the Chairman of the Anti-Libel Alliance (ALA), was exiting the Kenneth Myer Building at the University of Melbourne in Parkville. He had just given a lecture about a study produced by the Sol School of Neuroscience concerning the correlation between anti-system sentiment and neurological disorders like temporal lobe epilepsy.

He produced a Stradivarius Churchill Cigar from the inner pocket of his tailor made semi-bespoke navy blue suit jacket, lighting it with a match and pacing outside the building for several minutes as he drew back on the inviting creamy vanilla aroma of the vintage tobacco.

As he looked down at his android smartphone checking his

emails a masked assailant approached yelling "Hail Earl Pierce", firing three gunshots from a Yugoslavian Zastava M88 9mm revolver at Dr. Foxman, wounding him once in the right shoulder.

The assailant, who dropped the revolver by Dr. Foxman's side as he lay on the ground bleeding, quickly ran to a silver Toyota Camry parked on Royal Parade and sped off in the direction of Coburg.

Bystanders quickly ran to help Dr. Foxman and within less than ten minutes an ambulance and state police were on the scene of the shooting. Dr. Foxman was transported to the nearby Royal Melbourne Hospital.

By roughly 2:45pm Australian Federal Police (AFP) from the Melbourne office in LaTrobe Street were deployed to investigate the shooting as a possible terrorist attack.

The Toyota Camry, which was tracked via a series of closed-circuit television (CCTV) video surveillance cameras, had been found abandoned in Champ St, Coburg near the Pentridge shopping centre. It was also coincidentally a five minute walk from the National Electoral Committee offices that Lucas had visited some months prior.

Around 8:00pm that evening state and federal police claimed they had the two suspects responsible for the attempted assassination in custody. The two white eighteen year olds they had rounded up had underlying mental disorders, were near illiterate and denied knowing anything about the shooting.

By the next morning, with Dr. Foxman in stable condition,

system organisations had begun levelling a trove of press statements imploring the AFP and ASIO to act against the "clear and present danger" posed by the writer 'Earl Pierce' who had "maliciously incited this act of terror against the system".

Major General David Burgess, the Director-General of Security for ASIO, responded to these statements that had permeated throughout the 24 hour mainstream media news cycle with the following written statement:

"The Australian Security Intelligence Organisation (ASIO) will wholeheartedly defend the nation against all anti-system threats posed by far-right extremists and white supremacist terrorists. Yesterday's assassination attempt against Dr. Jonathan Foxman, the Chairman of the Anti-Libel Alliance (ALA), was an abhorrent attack and ASIO will be vigorously pursuing all individuals involved for this egregious assault against our multicultural liberal democracy."

Meanwhile Vincent had also published a public statement on behalf of Rek-Wiz-It on the magazine's website:

"Rek-Wiz-It magazine is deeply disturbed by this hurriedly investigation that has been conducted by the Australian Federal Police (AFP) which so far is reportedly singling out contributors of our publication as masterminds of this shooting incident.

Is the public sincerely meant to believe that a single gunshot wound in the right shoulder, which is on the opposite side of the body from where the heart is, committed only minutes away from a reputable hospital by two alleged assailants whom are so lacking in literacy skills that they can't even read our magazine a legitimate explanation?

It is the firm belief of Rek-Wiz-It magazine that this incident was in all likelihood a false flag operation carried out by system agents to frame our committed contributors and malign our valued readers."

ASIO were quick to put pressure on the internet hosting service that ran Rek-Wiz-It magazine's website servers to have the site taken offline, but not quick enough to prevent thousands of people mirroring a screenshot of Vincent's statement and reposting the written text of said statement across multiple social media platforms.

Other alternative hardcopy and electronic publications that the mainstream media dubbed as "far right" and "conspiracy theorist" were quick to proclaim solidarity with Vincent and Rek-Wiz-It.

Lucas in the meantime had been following the unfolding news from up North in Coffs Harbour. Taking to Maria's Italian Restaurant on Harbour Drive, Lucas and Joseph shared a pasta dinner to talk about what had transpired.

"Joseph mate I get the feeling the government goon squads are going to be coming after me over this latest shitshow," Lucas said.

"Brother if push comes to shove I have a plan you might be interested in," Joseph responded.

"What's that mate?" Lucas inquired.

"We can borrow my father's yacht and sail it up the coast,

then navigate it around the top end across to Indonesia. I have friends over there that belong to the Church that can put us up for a good while." Joseph outlined.

"Brilliant idea mate!" Lucas replied.

"There's always the option of taking our chances in Port Moresby, but Papua is a crime riddled outpost of the Commonwealth, and the Australian government have better relations with them than they do the Indonesians on account of the whole Muslim majority thing." Joseph explained.

"I foresee these system sycophants in Canberra being prepared to literally scalp us to appease their overlords. Thank almighty God that Mormons find more in common with Muslims than socially liberal hyperinflationary system types. Let me know the soonest we can take off for Indonesia," Lucas stated.

"Sure thing brother. What about Vincent, Jacob, Larissa and Emily?" Joseph asked.

"Vincent and Larissa aren't going to readily retreat offshore. Vincent is digging in to make a principled plea for freedom of speech. I'll get in touch with Jacob and Emily ASAP," Lucas replied.

As the two finished dinner, Lucas reflected on the fact that he was yet to have been publicly identified as the elusive 'Earl Pierce'. His family were wholly unaware of his publishing exploits and Lucas intended to keep it that way. Ignorance was not only bliss but plausible deniability.

That night Lucas sent an encrypted e-mail to Jacob and

Emily which read:

> *"Hi frens,*
> *J and I are taking a trip. Keep me posted about your*
> *plans.*
> *Regards,*
> *L*

Jacob and Emily received the message the next morning and were on the road by mid-afternoon the same day for Adelaide. Jacob sent Lucas an encrypted e-mail using the public Wi-Fi at McDonald's West Richmond restaurant on Marion Road stating:

> *"Hey L,*
> *E and myself got some inspiration from Redgum's*
> *March, 1984 single release.*
> *Will keep you guys posted.*
> *Regards,*
> *J*

Jacob and Emily spent the night at the Tequila Sunrise Hostel, which was about a thirteen minute drive away from the Adelaide airport. The next morning they booked a last minute flight to Bali that took off at midday via Jetstar airlines.

Meanwhile Vincent and Larissa had taken to bunkering down with friends in Greensborough, after black bloc anarchists had thrown a Molotov cocktail through the lounge room window at the front of their home.

Over the weekend as volume eleven of 'Revolt Against The Synarchist Vampires' was due to be sold at newsagencies across the state, Vincent received a call from his lawyer Mark Jameson.

"Vincent the Australian Classification Board and Minister for Communications have sent me letters that have outlined their immediate intention to ban all future publishing of Rek-Wiz-It magazine," Mark sternly stated.

"Why am I not surprised? What legal recourse do we have in challenging their decision mate?" Vincent asked.

"I'm going to have to make some inquiries with other legal colleagues over it, but it may take a couple of years through the courts before any decision like this is overturned," Mark replied.

"Mark mate keep me posted on this, we're not going to kowtow to these bureaucratic bastards!" Vincent heatedly stated.

Like Aldous Huxley's 'Brave New World', which had been banned in Australia from 1932 to 1937, the dystopian tale weaved by 'Earl Pierce' was being treated like literary terrorism by the Australian government.

With the U.S. Presidential Election only a few days away, pro- Drumpf trolls were trying to associate Rek-Wiz-It with the likes of Hamas and Hezbollah. They were hell-bent on ensuring that the anti-system "far-right" were to be divorced from Drumpf's candidacy before he took the White House.

At the time the focus of the "woke" New Left and their liberal allies were to frame the focus of Drumpf's support base as being manufactured by "Russian collusion". It wasn't until 2020 when previously sealed Federal Bureau of Investigation (FBI) documents were presented in legal proceedings that it was discovered that it had been in fact private pro-system intelligence agency collusion that had secured the presidency for Drumpf.

Meanwhile Lucas and Joseph had been packing to sail around to Indonesia. Lucas, who was accustomed to travelling light, was primarily focused on safeguarding his writing journals and laptop. Joseph, who was preparing for the worst-case scenario, had decided to bring all his bolt action rifles and shotguns with him.

Joseph's father Graham, who'd retired from the armed forces and held similar political views to his son, was eager to assist Joseph in journeying up to Indonesia. Graham had served in a close capacity with members of the LDS Church in carrying out humanitarian support in the region and knew Joseph was in good hands upon arrival in the country.

Loaning Joseph $30,000 in cash, Graham helped Joseph load up his Ford Falcon Ute with provisions for the voyage up the coast and proceeded to hug Joseph and say farewell. Joseph got in the vehicle waved to his father and drove off.

Joseph proceeded to pick up Lucas from John's place. John too was saying goodbye, as he and Lucas enjoyed a stubby each of Crown Larger on the back veranda.

"Lucas mate it's been a pleasure having you stay! Where you off to next?" John asked.

"Heading back South for a while," Lucas calculating stated.

The less John knew about Lucas' actual destination would benefit both of them.

Shaking hands and sharing a laugh as Lucas loaded up his bags into Joseph's ute, Lucas and John waved to each other as Lucas and Joseph drove off in the direction of the marina where Graham's Pacific Sea Craft 34 cruising yacht was in port.

Lucas and Joseph finished loading the boat up with supplies and luggage, and left Joseph's ute parked nearby the Harbourside Markets for Graham to come collect later after they'd left port. Before they shipped out Lucas took to a local cafe with public Wi-Fi and sent an encrypted e-mail to Vincent:

> *"Hey V,*
> *J and myself are taking your advice from August*
> *mate. Looking to catch up with J and E in about two*
> *months time. Will be in touch.*
> *Regards,*
> *L*

By noon Lucas and Joseph were ready to ship out. Joseph had calculated it would roughly take about twenty six to twenty eight days if cruising at an average of 4.6 knots. Lucas who didn't have a great deal of boating experience was happy taking sailing directions from Joseph, who he endearingly referred to as 'Captain Hyrum'.

By the time Drumpf had declared victory at the Hilton hotel in Midtown Manhattan, Jacob and Emily had secured a place of residence at Villa Puri Royan, a cheap three star hotel situated between Jimbaran Beach, Queen Beach and Kedonganan Beach. Thanks to a generous wire transfer from

Jacob's father they would be well off for some time.

Emily, who found it relatively easy to secure a hospitality job due to her work experience and aesthetic attractive features, began working in a fast paced bar as well as working as a yoga instructor. Networking with a confused mixture of spiritually craving misfits and tourists, Emily began to develop a tarot customer base from these jobs in which to offer her clairvoyant services to.

Jacob was able to find work as an artist for a screen printing business that designed trendy clothing for both domestic tourist sales and overseas export. He would soon be able to convince his employer to run production of the elaborate colourful prints he produced for 'Revolt Against The Synarchist Vampires'.

Taking up the habit of smoking Djarum Black clove cigarettes and drinking Manta's White Rum, Jacob spent his off hours drawing whilst musing in relief that he and Emily had managed to escape the immediate clutches of the Australian authorities for the moment.

Meanwhile Vincent was busy coordinating with his allies in the alternative press to drum up outrage propaganda against the Australian government. Having foreseen Rek-Wiz-it's banning, Vincent had already cunningly conjured up another logo and format design for a new magazine he had titled 'Stake Of Truth'.

With troves of new contributors bidding to be recruited over the next couple of months, the government's banning of Rek-Wiz-It would only help amplify Vincent's publishing endeavours. Come December 1st, 2016, a newly crafted

'Stake Of Truth' would make newsagency magazine shelves, with volumes eleven and twelve of 'Revolt Against The Synarchist Vampires' by 'Earl Pierce' being its prized feature content.

Lucas and Joseph had by this time lazily made their way up the coast along the Great Barrier Reef. Having spent their time conversing and writing between sailing duties, the two had only ported once thus far at Port Douglas in Queensland.

Both Lucas and Joseph were keen to make as few stops as possible in case certain prying eyes on land were to take an interest. By Monday 21st November Lucas and Joseph ported for the last time in Australia at Frances Bay in Darwin.

Using a public internet Wi-Fi access at a nearby hotel lobby, Lucas checked his e-mails one last time before he and Joseph traversed through the Timor Sea.
Vincent had sent Lucas an encrypted e-mail which read:

> *G'day L,*
> *Hope you two get out alright.*
> *We'll be fighting the good fight from here.*
> *Say hi to J and E for us.*
> *Regards,*
> *V*

Lucas proceeded to send an encrypted e-mail to Jacob to ascertain his and Emily's whereabouts once Joseph and Lucas docked in at Bali.

Over the next couple of days as they sailed out of Australian waters, being stopped only twice by Australian Patrol boats, Lucas and Joseph sighed in relief that they'd not been

detained by the authorities, nor had said authorities found
Joseph's hidden cache of firearms.

Tacking their way through the warm climate of the Timor Sea
into the Indian Ocean, Lucas and Joseph docked in at the Port
of Benoa on Saturday 3rd December at roughly 8am Central
Indonesia Time. Upon arriving Joseph went to change some
Australian dollars into local currency whilst Lucas stayed
near the yacht.

After paying to have their vessel docked in at the Port for
three months, Lucas and Joseph proceeded to unload their
luggage from the yacht into a Blue Bird taxi and make their
way to Central Park in Kuta, Bali where the branch of the
Church of Jesus Christ of Latter-day Saints was located.

Graham had notified Bishop I Wayan, who oversaw the
Bali branch, that his son Joseph and friend Lucas would be
arriving around the beginning of December. Anticipating
their arrival, Bishop I Wayan had readied a room at his home
nearby to the Church branch where the two travellers could
bunker down.

After Lucas and Joseph transported their belongings to their
temporary accommodation, the two lads took to a nearby
Hotel to check their e-mails. Jacob had replied to Lucas' in
an encrypted message:

> *Hi L,*
> *Villa Puri Royan Jl. Pantai Sari No.25, Jimbaran,*
> *Kec. Kuta Sel., Kabupaten Badung, Bali 80361,*
> *Indonesia*
> *Regards,*
> *J*

Commuting through the bustling streets of Bali once again via a Blue Bird taxi, Lucas and Joseph made the 8km journey to where Jacob and Emily were staying, arriving about noon at their destination. Lucas requested that reception notify them that they'd arrived.

Emily came to the front of the property to greet Lucas and Jacob.

"Hi guys, great to see you've made it here in one piece!" Emily said with delight.

"Great to see you too, Em! How's our buddy Jacob doing?" Lucas enquired.

"He's good. He'd been worried a bit after the shooting went down, but has been doing great with the change of scenery." Emily replied.

"Great to hear, sister!" Joseph said.

"Where's he at?" Lucas asked.

"He'll be back soon. He just went out to pick up a pack of Djarum Blacks," Emily replied.

As the three loitered in the reception chatting back and forth for several minutes Jacob appeared from the street.

"Hey lads, thought we might have lost you. How was the cruise from Coffs Harbour?" Jacob asked.

"Absolutely serene mate!" Lucas replied.

"Brilliant! We'll have to go out to celebrate your arrival," Jacob suggested.

"Good idea brother!" Joseph said.

The four of them walked five minutes around the block to AKUA de Bilbao Spanish restaurant and grabbed a table in sight of the beachfront ocean view. As they wined and dined on the shores of the Muslim majority nation they took solace in knowing the Indonesian government wouldn't be troubled by the shooting of Dr. Jonathan Foxman.

Considering a World Service Poll indicated that a staggering sixty four percent of Indonesian citizens viewed the socially liberal hyperinflationary system negatively compared to only nine percent expressing a positive view, it seemed for the moment they were in a space of sanctuary.

Chapter 5

A fortnight after Lucas and Joseph had arrived in Bali, the pair had managed to secure employment in order to sustain themselves whilst staying on the island. Lucas had found a job at a supersessionist church called the 'Community of Yeshua's New Covenant' working on maintenance and outreach projects and Joseph had found a good paying job as a videographer.

The two lads moved out of the room at Bishop I Wayan's home and moved into the Villa Puri Royan hotel to be close to Jacob and Emily. In the off hours the four compatriots diligently worked pumping out essays, articles and artwork for the newly minted Stake Of Truth magazine.

Meanwhile Vincent was busy tackling the ongoing shitshow emanating from the shooting of Dr. Jonathan Foxman. The state counter terrorism unit had charged Vincent with an Incitement offence and Mark Jameson was busy working to quash the charge.

Thanks to the recommendations of ASIO and The Australia System Affairs Council (ASAC), the Executive Council of Australian Systemisation (ECAS), the Anti-Libel Alliance (ALA) and the System Federation of Australia (SFA) federal legislation was being devised to circumvent further anti-system discourse.

Prime Minister Michael Trumble was busy seeking to fast-track a Religious Discrimination Bill and Anti-Trolling Bill through the Parliament and civil liberties groups were ostensibly turning a blind eye to the impacts these bills would have on citizen's speech rights.

However the impacts were not being lost in translation amongst the average citizens in Australia. The National Electoral Committee (NEC) was seeing a dramatic surge in new members and despite certain system attempts to have the party deregistered this membership surge was proving to be too hard to ignore.

System operatives had determined that the best course of strategy would be to initiate a supercharged dark public relations (DPR) campaign against the NEC leadership team with the intent of harming, discrediting and ultimately destroying their ability to operate.

The NEC was by no means unfamiliar with the system's DPR tactics as they were fluent in intelligence gathering and knew how to combat any attempt to divide the party.

Vanessa, who had not seen Lucas for some months, had sent him an e-mail outlining a request for support:

Dear Lucas,

The system has the National Electoral Committee in its crosshairs. Recent censorship legislation (i.e. The Religious Discrimination Bill 2016 and Anti Trolling Bill 2016) will be used to level vexatious lawfare against dissidents and political organisers whom are fed up with the system's speech suppression agenda.

We are making an appeal to our members to help us any way they can in combating the onslaught from these oligarchs and their plutocrat pets.

Please contact our national office to let us know what skill sets you can offer in this endeavour.

Sincerely,

Vanessa

Lucas, who was mindful of the fact that the intelligence community would likely be monitoring communications to and from the NEC headquarters, was keen to communicate to Vanessa that he was still fighting the good fight:

Dear Vanessa,

Please be advised that the National Electoral Committee has my utmost support.

Following a truism of Edward Bulwer-Lytton I will be taking up the might of the pen in challenging the sword of the state.

As I suspect the system's five eyes intelligence alliances will be monitoring our communication I will refrain from expressing where my writing will feature for the moment.

I'll be in touch soon!

Regards,

Lucas

Christmas was a few days away and this was the first one for some years in which Lucas wouldn't be spending it with his family members. He decided to make a call to his parents Jacinta and Scott, his sisters Sandra and Elise as well as his brother Jack.

Lucas told them all that he was out of the country with friends and would regrettably not be able to see them for the holidays. He only confided in Jack as to where exactly he was currently residing. Jack, who lived alone and had a good paying job as a master builder, communicated to Lucas that he'd book a flight to Bali after New Years to spend Australia Day with him.

Lucas, Joseph, Jacob and Emily prepared to celebrate the holidays together on the neighbouring beaches to the hotel. Dining out on a seafood feast at the Jimbaran Beach Cafe, they all exchanged small practical gifts with one another, such as art materials, manta rum and t-shirts.

They spent Christmas evening trekking through the cool waters that collided with the shore, taking turns behind the lens of a digital camera capturing the good times spent in numerous photos. As night set in, Jacob and Emily walked to the southern point of Jimbaran Beach to peruse the clubs and bars, whilst Lucas and Joseph had a gelato from a nearby ice creamy and retired back to their room at Villa Puri Royan to read.

Back in Ivanhoe Vincent and Larissa were spending the night celebrating with Vincent's brother Tom over a home style mixed vegetable curry dinner.

"Vincent bro, how's the new publishing project going?" asked Tom.

"Not bad bro, Stake Of Truth looks to be overtaking New Dawn, Nexus, Uncensored and Quadrant in sales," Vincent replied.

"It'd be nice if the counter terrorism unit could get their boots off our back!" Larissa interjected.

"I wouldn't worry too much about it guys, there's so many people sick to death of this woke political correctness crap that I don't readily see them having much success in realistically implementing these latest bills without significantly beefing up police powers," Tom stated.

"I wouldn't put such a move past them bro, but I agree it's a risky move when so many are readying for rebellion against the system at the moment." Vincent replied

Sharing a sparkling rose wine over a raspberry cheesecake dessert Vincent, Larissa and Tom chatted into the late hours about family, friends and future endeavours. The niggling charge of Incitement blurred into the background of their thoughts for at least a brief moment as they enjoyed the aura of the holiday.

Over the week that stretched from Christmas to New Years a series of mainstream media articles were published about a "satanic Nazi paramilitary group". One particular article titled "Terrorist Group Incited by Subversive Story" disseminated by The Epoch and Sydney Afternoon Messenger postulated that:

"A far-right propagandist going by the alias 'Earl Pierce' has been determined by state and federal law-enforcement to be the source of inspiration for a domestic terrorist group going by the name of 'Van Helsing Division'.

'Revolt Against The Synarchist Vampires' an apocalyptic subversive serialised work of fiction written by 'Earl Pierce' has reportedly been characterised by the Occult Operations Executive (OOE) to be a "blue print for far-right white supremacists to wage a guerrilla war against our righteous inclusive system of government."

The Occult Operations Executive (OOE) was a special ASIO department tasked with Psychological Operations (psyop) that utilised occult methods to manufacture and fracture system enemies with varying degrees of "evidence" of actual threat and violence being perpetrated by said enemies.

Coordinating a multi-front operational offensive with "parapsychology tactics" to overwhelm targets, the OOE was tasked with providing governments a mock mandate to install emergency actions, such as via national security legislation. This provided the state with the necessary pretext to inflict force and violence against the population with ostensible legal impunity.

Vincent, who regularly read through the daily mainstream media newspapers to gauge where the system was seeking to herd the bewildered masses into, had honed in on this article about the mysterious 'Van Helsing Division'. Apart from some edgy propaganda using a standardised graphic design layout, which coincidentally began showing up in online forums around the same time as Dr. Jonathan Foxman's shooting, ostensibly no one had heard of the group.

Vincent drafted a letter from the editor to be published in the January edition of Stake Of Truth which read as follows:

> *Dear Readers,*
> *We are currently experiencing a concerted effort by the Australian intelligence community to see Stake Of Truth magazine shut-down and its contributors put behind bars.*
>
> *According to reports by the system media cartels a serialised work of literary truth published in our pages is allegedly responsible for a mysterious "terrorist group" purportedly called "Van Helsing Division" that has sprung up in the last month.*
>
> *Far be it for your humble editor to suggest that this group is being armed, trained and/or organised by the intelligence community itself, but as there is significant precedent for that to be the case this editor is not ruling out such conclusions.*
>
> *Please be advised that I will be offering $10,000 reward for any member of the public who can*

substantiate a link between "Van Helsing Division"
and the intelligence community in Australia.

Sincerely,

Vincent Tynan
Editor

Sensing there may be a crackdown on the magazine before it could go to print, Vincent circulated the letter to as many alternative media and mainstream media outlets as possible. Within days of the letter being sent, Vincent's words had thoroughly made the rounds before Stake Of Truth was successfully being churned out of the printing press on New Year's Eve.

Meanwhile Lucas, Joseph, Jacob and Emily had trekked the two hour walk to Seminyak Beach for the New Year's Eve fireworks. Dinning out on Spanish tapas and knocking back bottled brem, rum and fruit juice at the La Plancha beachfront restaurant the four of them saw in the beginning of 2017 beneath an illuminated night sky filled with colourful explosions.

On their southward walk back to the motel the four compatriots were approached by an English speaking Balinese man named Kadek.

"Greetings Lucas, Joseph, Jacob and Emily. My name is Kadek, I'm an expert staffer specialising in politics and ideology for the Indonesian state intelligence agency Badan Intelijen Negara (BIN)" Kadek stated.

"Are we in trouble with your government?" Lucas asked.

"No quite the contrary. We are eager to offer you and your colleagues an office to run your propaganda operation from," Kadek replied.

"How do you know about our publishing exploits?" Jacob asked.

"A search of your rooms was carried out when cleaning staff came across firearms in one of your rooms." Kadek explained.

"Will you be seizing the firearms?" Joseph asked.

"Only if you refuse our offer" Kadek replied in a nonchalant way.

Kadek walked and talked with the four compatriots on their way back to the motel, discussing the sorts of facilities and resources the BIN could deliver in aiding them with the Stake Of Truth operation.

It wasn't made crystal clear by Kadek that the BIN were aware of the Australian media's manufactured correlation between their publication and the Dr. Foxman false flag, but Lucas innately knew this was the agency's motivation to lend support to them.

Kadek provided Lucas with a business card for a printing company that produced flyers and several newsprint tourist papers. On the back of the business card Kadek had scrawled a mobile number where they could make contact with his department.

Over the next week, whilst Stake Of Truth was hitting the magazine shelves in newsagencies across the country, the four of them moved their makeshift art studio at Villa Puri Royan motel to three offices at the back of Luar Biasa Printing Pty Ltd which was roughly ten minutes walking distance away.

One of the offices, which had previously served as a staff break room for night shift press workers, had an en suite and bed in it. As Luar Biasa Printing Pty Ltd was only five minutes walk from where Lucas worked at the 'Community of Yeshua's New Covenant' church he decided to move into the office to be closer to the congregation.

Meanwhile Lucas's brother Jack was readying to ship out to Bali. Jack lived in Barangaroo, Sydney and was only a twenty minute drive from the Sydney airport. Taking a taxi to the T1 International drop-off, Jack made his way through airport processing and boarded a midday non-stop flight to Bali via Garuda Indonesia airline.

Enjoying a comfortable six and half hour flight, Jack landed in Bali that evening and made his way to the Hilton Garden Inn near Ngurah Rai Airport. He e-mailed Lucas of his arrival in Bali and settled in for the night. Lucas received Jack's e-mail around 8 am the next morning and trekked the forty-five minute walk to Jack's hotel arriving around 11 am.

"Hey bro, how was your flight?" Lucas asked as he gave Jack a hug.

"Great bro! They played 'A cure for wellness' on the flight over, Jack replied.

"Nice! How did Christmas go with the family?" Lucas asked.

"It was okay. Lauren and Rachel were quite the handful. Elise has got a new job working for the South Australian government as an analyst," Jack replied.

"Good on her! How about mum and dad?" Lucas asked.

"They've been missing you bro. When you coming back?" Jack asked.

"Playing it by year at the moment, we've had a little opportunity open up that'll keep us occupied for awhile," Lucas replied.

Lucas and Jack continued chatting back and forth as they waved down a Blue Bird taxi to head 11km to the flea market in Kuta between Petitenget beach and Seminyak beach. Whilst perusing the vibrantly arranged stalls surrounded by the intertwining scents of fennel, ginger, coconut and peanuts Jack purchased from a vendor a bag of dried psilocybin mushrooms and some bottles of brem.

The two brothers walked to the shoreline of the nearby beach and starred out across the glistening waves that caught the shimmering rays of sunlight. As they lay back on the sand sipping the fermented rice wine waiting for the kaleidoscope effects of the mushrooms to take hold Lucas and Jack joked and laughed as the two of them goofily sang 'White Rabbit' by Jefferson Airplane.

Over the next five hours as the early afternoon descended into the early evening the two brothers found themselves drawn to a restaurant called La Favela where they diligently

scoffed down tacos and swigged Bintang beers. By 8pm
Lucas and Jack had made their way into the back of a Blue
Bird taxi once again and were heading back to Hilton Garden
Inn. Lucas, who couldn't be bothered journeying back to
his room at Luar Biasa Printing Pty Ltd, decided to crash in
Jack's room which had twin beds overlooking the pool.

The next morning Lucas and Jack went for breakfast at The
Garden Grille, a restaurant which was a part of the hotel.
With an aperitif of gin and a spread of poached eggs, grilled
houmani, grilled button mushrooms, grilled eggplant and
chicken sausages the two enjoyed a hot meal before Lucas
was to take off for work.

Assuring Jack they'd touch base later that day Lucas trekked
from the hotel to his workplace. Arriving at around 11am
Lucas was greeted by Pastor Steven Hewitt, the American
born leader of the Community of Yeshua's New Covenant
church, who was eager to speak with him.

"Lucas our affiliate churches have contacted me with a
proposal for a printed periodical that promotes our soul
winning message. I recall you having said that you have
previous experience in this sort of work?" Pastor Hewitt
enquired.

"I do indeed, Pastor Hewitt!" Lucas affirmed.

"Praise Him! I'd be able to handle the editorial work
relating to written submissions from our contributors, we're
wondering if you could help with typesetting, formatting,
artwork and such?" Pastor Hewitt further asked.

"Count me in!" Lucas exclaimed.

Chapter 6

"Damn homo whore!" Vincent yelled at the television.

Prime Minister Michael Trumble was announcing via a nationally televised press conference that his government would be initiating an "inquiry into anti-system extremists" in order to pursue a "facts on the ground" approach to facilitating a "final demise to the Whiteness problem".

"This scourge will stop! It is not enough for our government to merely suspend habeas corpus and intern these hate filled evil doers, we must rely on more fatal solutions!" Trumble sternly stated.

Cheered on by an elated press gallery consisting of wine guzzling feminists, liberals and pretentious promiscuous perverts, Trumble further outlined in so many words that he wouldn't rule out deploying the military domestically in securing an "honourable peace".

"This system serving cocksucker isn't going to be happy until he can legally bathe in the blood of Simon of Trent!" Vincent growled.

"What's the next plan of attack, hun?" Larissa asked.

"In the words of Sun Tzu; hold out baits to entice the enemy. Feign disorder, and crush him. Do not swallow bait offered by the enemy. Do not interfere with an army that is returning home. Great results, can be achieved with small forces," Vincent recited.

Vincent's eighty pen wielding keyboard warriors contributing to his publications were fluent in the communication skills required for an effective troll farm. With the government postulating these "anti-system extremists" to be "evil doers" whilst the system itself engages in wars, espionage, sabotage and corruption it was easy enough to judo flip the system's inversion of reality into a propaganda plan of persuasion.

Meanwhile Lucas had fallen asleep on the wooden pew of the 'Community of Yeshua's New Covenant' church during a sleep over with young adult parishioners and elders of the congregation. They'd been working on a brainstorming committee pertaining to their new church periodical which they'd agreed to name 'Reflections Upon Truth'.

Having bundled up his shirt as a pillow and laying down topless, Lucas had managed to sleep five hours when he awoke to parishioners making tea and coffee. He poured himself some fruit juice and drank it down quickly before politely parting with his church friends.

Lucas trekked the five minutes back to Luar Biasa Printing

Pty Ltd where Joseph, Jacob and Emily were busy at work getting copy ready for next month's issue of 'Stake Of Truth'.

"Hey guys, how we looking for next month's content?" Lucas asked.

"Good as gold mate!" Jacob answered.

"We got an e-mail from Vincent this morning, brother," Joseph said.

"What did it say?" Lucas inquired.

"He suggested Earl Pierce summon some inspired words for those in the Australian army. We need to forewarn them that if they cast off their covenant with God for an oath to criminals and tyrants they'd better forearm for the torment of outer darkness," Joseph outlined.

"I'll see what I can muster up. I'll probably need to go back and edit some of the existing copy I've already typed up," Lucas replied.

Emily was busy working on a realist sketch for Joseph's latest essay titled the "The Theocracy of Whiteness" which depicted both a clean cut white shirted worker and white shirted bishop contrasted with shadowy personages draped in black bloc and a black bekishe. In the essay Joseph proposed to the reader that when it came to an allegiance with Whiteness and an allegiance with the current system it was an either/or situation.

Jacob had been working on the cover art for the next month's issue of 'Stake Of Truth'. It depicted a loyal organiser from the pages of 'Revolt Against The Synarchist Vampires' sitting in the foreground at a desk writing with a pen whilst in the background was a romanticised apparition of said loyal organiser wielding a sword with outspread angelic wings.

"I think Vincent is beginning to have some truthful visions as to where the government is heading at the moment" Jacob aptly stated.

"Holy war?" Lucas asked in jest.

"Well as the Zen Buddhist master said, "We'll see." I get the feeling things are going to heat up soon enough," Jacob replied.

Lucas walked into the nearby room where he was residing and opened his laptop. Before going over his notes for 'Revolt Against The Synarchist Vampires' and making revisions to the plot Lucas noted that Jack had sent through an e-mail:

> *Hey bro,*
> *Want to catch up for dinner tonight?*
> *Jack*

Lucas promptly wrote back that he'd catch him tonight around 6:00pm at Warung Mufu Balinese Foods & Pork Ribs which was a two minute walk from Jack's hotel. Lucas needed the day to start refining his serialised story that had garnered such notoriety in Australia.

Lucas had gone to great lengths in his writing to tactically weaponise deception by applying Sun Tzu's axiom of

"Appear weak when you are strong, and strong when you are weak."

The "legions" of loyal organisers had ostensibly created a widespread underground network whose cultic milieu manifested as a sort of cross between the movie 'They Live' mixed with the idyllic religious aesthetic depicted in David Lindsley's Mormon church paintings.

Far from being the sorts of mountain dwelling Castro tier revolutionaries battling Batista from afar via radio broadcasts, the loyal organisers were an on the ground force much like the Sicarii, Werwolf resistance or Red Army Faction (aka Baader–Meinhof Group).

Disseminating compelling propaganda that played to confirmation bias and cognitive-dissonance in order to undermine and demystify the multifaceted "mind game" of the trillioniare tyranny, loyal organisers were able to "dehypnotize" and mobilize.

The loyal organisers professed a message pertaining to the spiritual that was akin to what Francis Galton stipulated for the biological (i.e. Eugenics). Citing Matthew 19:24 from the New Testament of the Bible as the foundation of their views, they postulated that the "superior stock of spirits" were antithetical to the trillioniare tyrants whom blasphemously served plutocracy and plunder.

Lucas, by the pen of 'Earl Pierce', wrote:

"With Truth as their weapon the Loyal Organisers did command the grunts in the standing army, whom had swore an oath to a crown of blood soaked gold, to free themselves

from the bondage of manufactured fallacy and serve the righteous royals whom were temporally poor."

Joseph, who'd poked his head in to read what Lucas had written, encouraged Lucas to qualify their weapon of Truth with a paraphrasing of 1 Nephi 16:2 from The Book of Mormon which stated:

"And it came to pass that I said unto them that I knew that I had spoken hard things against the wicked, according to the truth; and the righteous have I justified, and testified that they should be lifted up at the last day; wherefore, the guilty taketh the truth to be hard, for it cutteth them to the very center."

Lucas agreed the sentiment of the verse provoked the desired effect which was needed for the next edition of the story. He further reinforced Joseph's suggested verse from The Book of Mormon with a direct citation of Romans 1:18 from the New Testament which stated:

"The wrath of God is being revealed from heaven against all the godlessness and wickedness of people, who suppress the truth by their wickedness,"

As 6:00pm neared Lucas had ostensibly finished his revised copy of 'Revolt Against The Synarchist Vampires' and had e-mailed it to Vincent and the dozen other alternative media outlets that that had agreed to disseminate it amongst the pages of their publications.

By the time Lucas reached Warung Mufu Balinese Foods & Pork Ribs to meet Jack it was 6:23pm.

"Sorry I'm a tad late bro, have been working hard on this project at the minute and lost track of time" Lucas stated apologetically.

"No sweat bro, just been having a couple of beers. What are you drinking?" Jack asked.

"I'll have a Manta rum and coke," Lucas replied.

As Lucas and Jack chatted back and forth about general matters pertaining to family, friends and work Jack honed in on what it was that Lucas was currently doing with himself in Bali.

"So what brought you to Indonesia for work bro? Wasn't there enough of it in Australia?" Jack asked in jest.

"No bro, it's a long story. Migrated over with some mates and working with a church group at the minute. Also you gotta' admit the scenery is pretty beaut," Lucas replied.

"Yeah beautiful when bombings aren't happening," Jack joked.

Lucas was still reluctant to confide in Jack that he was part of an exiled propaganda operation now receiving support from the Indonesian state intelligence agency. The two brothers dug into a delicious feast of spit-roasted suckling pig (babi guling) and drank away the night as they reminisced and forecasted what the future may hold.

As the night came to an end Lucas and Jack were about to part ways when Jack stated "Hey bro, why don't I walk you back to your place?"

Lucas quickly responded by saying "No bro, I'm a forty-five minute walk away you're just over there."

"Alright, but e-mail me your address and I'll come to you next time," Jack responded.

Lucas agreed and began to walk away whilst waving to Jack. On the walk home Lucas decided to send Jack the address to Villa Puri Royan rather than his backroom at Luar Biasa Printing Pty Ltd. He didn't want Jack's eyebrow to raise over the whereabouts of his residence.

By this time Vincent had been contacted by multiple vlogger personalities, political commentators and video streamers to do interviews with regards to the newly purported crack down on "anti-system extremists".

Taking advantage of several offers Vincent booked up the next couple of weeks to face prying questions that would illuminate his autodidactic punditry on the matter of "anti-system extremism" and what Prime Minister Trumble termed the "Whiteness problem".

The first interview was scheduled to be held the next day at a makeshift studio in North Melbourne run by political commentator and YouTuber David Roper whose channel was titled 'Radical Roper Report'. David was noted as being a prolific "conspiracy theorist" and "pathological anti-system" propagandist.

It was safe to say Vincent's first interview was one void of adversity.

Vincent arrived at David's studio around 1pm and swiftly sat down for a coffee in the green room with the producers of the show. David's show would often run for four hours a day and had an eclectic line-up of in studio and teleconference guests.

David was a fast talking tangent spinning orator who was often prone to talking over guests in a fit of excitement and emotion. Vincent who was well versed in being concise and direct knew how to use David's energy to have the point land on target.

By about 1:45pm, whilst sponsor advertisements were playing over the live program feed, Vincent was brought out to sit down in the proverbial "hot seat" across from David.

"G'day Vincent mate, glad to have you on the show! We'll be going live again in a minute or two just hang in there" David stated in an emphatic upbeat fashion.

"Cheers David, will do," Vincent said.

As the advertisements finished up the technical crew for the 'Radical Roper Report' focused the lens of two expensive video cameras back on David.

"Welcome back brothers and sisters to the frontline of resistance against the kleptocratic kritarchy that is seeking to buy your precious souls with thirty pieces of silver. We know we are under attack and no-one knows this better than my next guest Vincent Tynan who is the editor and chief of 'Stake Of Truth' magazine and former editor of the outlawed dissident publication Rek-Wiz-It magazine... Vincent welcome!" David stated with exuberance.

"Thanks for having me David!" Vincent responded in a solemn upbeat fashion.

"Now tell us what is it at the crux of this criminal cancer that is killing our nation, raping our families, perverting our morals, stealing our sensibilities and subverting our life and liberty?" David energetically asked.

"In short it is the anti-Christ, anti-White, anti-human system that is governing over us as we speak!" Vincent sincerely replied.

"And how exactly are they achieving this Vincent? Is it through fifth dimensional warfare? Psycho-surgeries? Weaponized degeneracy? Mass drugging? Mainlined bioweapons? Toxic chemical airdrops from the sky? Polluting our drinking supply? Just what is it exactly is the plan of this nefarious cabal that rules us?" David yet again asked energetically.

"Well their plan consists of all of that and more!" Vincent emphatically replied.

"Tell us more Vincent... are they trying to summon interdimensional entities and demons to psychically occupy this world with powers of persuasion that will cause us to perceive their evil as good and our good as evil?" David once again asked.

"You hit the nail on the proverbial head David! What we are witnessing is a multifaceted mind game designed to enrich their exploitation, enshrine their warped inverted exaltation of sin and weaponize contradiction," Vincent sternly remarked.

"Can you explain the weaponization of contradiction further, Vincent?" David asked.

"Their logic is every idea contains its own contradiction and because God is the sum of all ideas He is posited as containing all contradictions. As they blasphemously considered themselves to be exalted to the status of God they believe they dictate the limits and infinite on what is regarded to be good and evil, true and false, healthy and sick" Vincent outlined.

"I see. So what is it that you think has caused them to frame your publications as the sum of all evil, falsehood and sickness?" David inquired.

"We have been a thorn in their side for some time. However a particular serialised fictional story we have been publishing has proved to be the proverbial straw that broke the camel's back" Vincent stated.

"And this serialised story I assume is 'Revolt Against The Synarchist Vampires' by the elusive author Earl Pierce?" David further asked.

"Yes, Earl Pierce has become a censured hate figure by those he refers to as the "trillioniare tyrants" who persecute, plunder and profit against the humble citizens," Vincent outlined.

"So can you tell us more..." David stated before being interrupted by a cue card from the show's producers that read "YouTube has shutdown the livestream."

"Sorry Vincent we're going to have to stop here for a moment it appears the overlords at YouTube has cut our feed," David lamented.

"Imagine my shock, David!" Vincent sarcastically stated.

"We'll have to leave it here for today whilst we sort this out. Thanks for coming in brother!" David stated energetically.

Vincent and David shook hands and parted ways. As Vincent exited the building and walked to his Ford Ranger several black bloc anarchist street criminals quickly approached him from behind and knocked him to the ground. They repeatedly and cowardly kicked Vincent whilst he lay on the ground in the foetal position in an attempt to protect himself from the beating.

Before they departed they poured a milk container of lambs blood over Vincent and ran away like demonic mongrel ferals. Whilst it was hard to discern that which was Vincent's blood and that which had been poured on him one thing was clear; the foot soldiers of the establishment had devolved from darting forked tongues and gnashing of teeth to outright bloody violence in broad daylight.

It was clear that the censorship campaign against the "White and delightsome" was beginning to accelerate across not only all media platforms but in the streets also.

Chapter 7

Lucas and Jack were having lunch at Kayumanis Resto Jimbaran, which was a twelve-minute walk from Villa Puri Royan. Lucas was eating a Balinese vegetable curry (aka Sayur Kare) with coconut rice and a bottle of Bintang beer whilst Jack ate chicken satay with Indonesian peanut sauce (aka Sate Ponorogo) as he sipped away at a lowball glass of Drum green label whisky.

"Bro I'm heading back Tuesday next week before Australia Day" Jack said.

"Righto bro, we'll make the best of the days you have left here!" Lucas exclaimed.

"How you holding up with cash reserves for yourself?" Jack asked.

"Not a problem, sorted for a good while at the moment" Lucas stated.

"Can I convince you to grab a ticket with me back to Sydney?" Jack asked invitingly.

"Can't do it just yet, have some pressing projects need addressing" Lucas said.

"Just think it over until I leave" Jack stated as he lightly whacked Lucas on the side of his left upper arm.

The two brothers were nearly finished eating when Jacob came hurriedly up to their table.

"Lucas mate we've got an issue at the office" Jacob stressed.

"Okay, be with you in two secs mate" Lucas responded.

Jacob swiftly walked back out to the front of the restaurant whilst Lucas and Jack wound up lunch.

"Bro I'll email you later" Lucas said

"Okay bro, hope it's nothing too serious. I'll sort the bill out." Jack stated.

"Cheers I owe you!" Lucas assuredly said.

The two brothers shook hands and Lucas quickly made his way out of the restaurant to where Jacob was waiting.

"Hey Jacob, what's the emergency?" Lucas asked.

"Kadek has said some CIA tier glow in the darks have been poking around about us via some NGO called Radio Free Encounter" Jacob outlined.

"Well that means the bloody ASIO mob know about us. Does Joseph and Emily know yet?" Lucas lamented and asked.

"I've told Emily. Joseph was out when I got the rundown" Jacob said.

Lucas and Jacob made their way over to Luar Biasa Printing Pty Ltd where Emily was situated. They waited for Joseph until he rocked up around 3:45pm.

The four of them discussed their strategy going forward. Stay in Bali and avoid being invited to a house in a remote suburb where they'd be later found in a trunk full of bullets from a suppressed automatic pistol or take a boat ride back into the belly of the beast (i.e. Australia).

"I say we take our chances here. The state intelligence agency has our backs and we have these premises to work out of" Jacob said.

"Well for the moment that is. What happens when the Indonesians want to sell us out to the yanks for a matter of convenience?" Emily asked.

"Joseph do you know any LDS in the CIA recruitment pipeline?" Lucas asked with a hint of tease.

"Though it's true they do recruit from our church I don't know anyone openly on the CIA payroll" Joseph said with an equal amount of jest.

"I propose we take a trip on the yacht back to Australia before the option is closed to us. We don't want to die in exile like Napoleon did on Saint Helena" Lucas said.

"Well the docking fees are covered till the end of next month so assumedly departure won't be an issue if we all wanted to leave" Joseph outlined.

"Emily and I can stay here until Kadek cuts the support and puts us on a plane ride back to Australia. If you guys want to ship back make sure to keep a low profile" Jacob cautioned.

"Joseph we'll start packing ourselves up and ship out on Thursday next week" Lucas said.

"That's Australia Day, such a poetic departure date" Joseph observed.

"It'll give me time to spend with Jack before he flies out" Lucas stated

The four compatriots began to prep for Lucas' and Joseph's departure in six-days time. Lucas e-mailed Jack to see if they could meet up at the Wanaku Seafood & Chinese Restaurant which was an eleven-minute walk from Jack's hotel. Jack replied within half hour and the two met up around 7:00pm.

"Jack I was giving some thought to what you said earlier about coming back to Australia with you. Joseph and I have some thing's to sort out first but we'll be coming back in the next couple of weeks" Lucas said.

"That's great to hear bro!" Jack exclaimed.

"I'm going to need the next two days to get the ball rolling on this. We'll meet up again on Tuesday, yeah?" Lucas asked.

"Sure thing bro. Let's just enjoy the rest of the evening for the moment" Jack stated.

Lucas still didn't want Jack to know that the reason why he wasn't getting on the plane home with his brother was because Joseph and he hadn't entered the country in the unconventional sense and didn't have passports which reflected their legal entry into the country.

The two brothers wined and dined for a couple of hours in a celebratory fashion. As they parted for the night Lucas and Jack agreed to catch up in three days time whilst Lucas sorted out his work commitments with the church.

Meanwhile Vincent had been discharged from hospital with various bruises, breaks and fractures. The blindsided attack on him by cowardly masked black bloc ferals had promptly been solemnly reported by the alternative media in Australia and some foreign outlets, whilst the mainstream media disseminated apologist propaganda for the "brave anti-fascists" who had assaulted him.

The Australia System Affairs Council (ASAC), the Executive Council of Australian Systemisation (ECAS), the Anti-Libel Alliance (ALA) and the System Federation of Australia (SFA) all produced near identical press releases that stated that:

"The direct action exacted against the White Supremacist anti-system terrorist Vincent Tynan is pure unadulterated social justice! We hope everyone like Mr. Tynan, particularly his devotees in 'Van Helsing Division', meets a similar fate in the days, weeks, months and years ahead!"

A day after these press releases were circulated by the mainstream media Vincent and Larissa's house was once again targeted with a Molotov cocktail.

In response Vincent directed his solicitor Mark Jameson to prompt Victoria police to press charges of criminal incitement against the CEOs of ASAC, ECAS, ALA and SFA. He also instructed Mark to pursue civil lawsuits of libel against all these organisations for defaming him as a "terrorist".

Three days later the incitement charges that had been put against Vincent the month prior were mysteriously quashed. It seemed the sacred system cows who'd sought to sacrifice Vincent as a crucified scapegoat had fool heartedly overplayed their audacity and self-confidence. Whilst Vincent had no illusions that any of these CEOs would be hit-up with incitement indictments he was hopeful that he would secure civil rulings of defamation against these organisations.

By this time Lucas, having worked a Monday morning on a hall painting project, had met up with Pastor Steven Hewitt to explain what was going on.

"Pastor Hewitt I've been called back home to Australia rather urgently regarding some personal matters. I'll be leaving Thursday" Lucas stated.

"Sorry to hear you are leaving us Lucas. Will you be seeking to get in touch with our affiliate churches when you get back?" Pastor Hewitt asked.

"Absolutely and don't worry I'll still be able to help you and the congregation out with the design work for the

'Reflections Upon Truth' journal! It's just going to be more e-mail centred rather than face-to-face" Lucas reassured.

"Thank-you Lucas, we greatly appreciate that!" Pastor Hewitt said gratefully.

Lucas and Pastor Hewitt went for a pasta lunch at Gourmet Garage restaurant and chatted about connecting Lucas up with a 'Community of Yeshua's New Covenant' church back in Australia.

Joseph had meanwhile secured his final paycheque from the video editing company he had been working for and, with monies from Lucas and Jacob, was spending the last days in Bali perusing the markets for supplies. By Tuesday afternoon Joseph had the yacht decked-up with provisions to get him and Lucas back to Australia.

Lucas and Jack met up at noon on Tuesday and spent the afternoon going between the beach and the bars, pacing themselves with their alcohol consumption. Come 7:30pm Lucas had Jack back at the Hilton Garden Inn, near Ngurah Rai Airport, so he could get ready to board his 10:35pm flight back to Sydney that night.

"Bro I hope you had a ripper time" Lucas said.

"Sure did bro! I guess the next time I'll be seeing you will be back home?" Jack rhetorically asked.

"Don't worry, bro! Have a safe flight back and I'll be seeing you soon" Lucas said in reassurance.

Lucas and Jack gave each other a brotherly hug and parted

ways. As scheduled Jack caught his nonstop six-hour flight back to Sydney without any issues arising.

On Wednesday Lucas and Joseph strategized the journey home. Praying they'd have as smoother sailing experience as they did on the trip to Bali, they agreed retracing the voyage previously travelled was the best course of action. Alternatively, the option of sailing down to Fremantle Harbour and commuting across country left them with the dilemma of getting Graham's yacht back to Coffs Harbour.

That evening Lucas, Joseph, Jacob and Emily went out for a seafood dinner at the New Moon Cafe situated on the South end of Kedonganan Beach. They knocked back Bintang beers and toasted to a safe journey for Lucas and Joseph the following day.

"Hopefully we'll be seeing you fellas again soon!" Jacob said.

"Hear, hear brother!" Joseph exclaimed.

"Will you guys need help getting down to the port tomorrow?" Emily asked.

"Best we don't all congregate near the yacht. Don't want to draw any more attention to our departure than what may already be the case" Lucas stated.

That evening after they retired back to the residence at the Villa Puri Royan, Joseph gave Jacob a Stevens 555 shotgun for having provided him and Lucas funds for provisions. Jacob, unbeknownst to Joseph, had also procured a .32 automatic colt pistol from a bar contact Jacob had met through Emily.

The next morning around 9:30am Lucas and Joseph discreetly made their way to the Port of Benoa to take their leave from the Indonesian shores. Without any prying eyes descending on them they sailed out of the harbour and into the Bali sea and then onto the Indian Ocean.

By this time Vincent and Larissa had once again bunkered down at Tom's place due to certain heated exchanges occurring outside their home in Ivanhoe. Despite this inconvenience, Vincent had been continuing to undertake interviews with alternative media outlets sporting a black eye and fractured left arm.

Addressing the convenient surge in spurious Neo-Nazi graffiti (i.e. distorted swastikas) and equally bogus "hate crimes" pertaining to ludicrous allegations of nooses being placed around celebrity necks and flyers being put in journalist mailboxes, Vincent repeatedly said:

"These egregiously false 'hate hoaxes' are routinely being perpetrated by system whores whom wish to virtue signal to their sordid tyrannical masters for praise and privileges. As in one documented case where one of these lunatics actually stabbed themselves and then reporting it to police as an "assault" perpetrated by a "gang" of "Nazis" it is clear these pro-system demons will stop at nothing to frame up their enemies."

Larissa, who was steadfastly supportive of Vincent's zeal to battle the system's tactics of suppression, was diligently working behind the scenes to help keep their assorted businesses on track. Thanks to a malicious mass reporting campaign to the Australian Taxation Office (ATO) by anonymous persons seeking to instigate an audit of their businesses, it was clear the system cabal was once again trying another route of harassment or means by which to inflict ruin upon them.

Vincent and Larissa addressed the rising stresses by taking a trip to a Tibetan Buddhist meditation centre North West of the city outside the regional town of Eaglehawk in Myers Flat. They stayed four nights at the Eaglehawk Motel, setting them back roughly $500, and would venture thirteen minutes up the road by vehicle to The Great Stupa of Universal Compassion.

Walking through the vibrant gardens displaying statues, prayer wheels and water features, as well as the surrounding bush terrain of the magnificent spiritual epicentre, Vincent and Larissa reflected on the troubles that were surrounding them. They contemplated whether to kowtow to the top-down pressures causing them grief or pursue their convictions with passion and humility.

Over a vegetarian curry lunch at the Stupaview Cafe on the second day of their stay they both decidedly were empowered to push on in their mission.

Meanwhile Lucas and Joseph had sailed the equivalent of the width of Victoria and were nearing the Timor Sea. As the sun set to the stern of the yacht the two friends feasted on a dish of nasi goreng prepared by Lucas and sipped on a Balinese herbal drink called loloh (which Joseph had enjoyed whilst his compatriots partook of brem and Bintang beer).

As Joseph took a few hours sleep, Lucas manned the yacht

as best he could whilst mindfully ready to wake Joseph if they began to drift off course.

About two and a half hours after Joseph had drifted the winds began to mysteriously die down. Lucas peered over the bow of the yacht and saw white flames burning above the sea surface.

All of a sudden the Holy Spirit softly spoke to Lucas by saying:
"Lucas, upon arriving back in your homeland visit your friend Caleb. Stay with him for three nights then seek out your acquaintances Amanda and Geoff. Geoff will offer you refuge at a small house in the town of Benalla. There I will set you forth an inspired task of writing a letter for the people of Australia. When you have completed it send it to your friend Vincent. Travel back to the city and stay with Amanda whom will offer you a room to stay."

The flames extinguished and the voice faded.

Lucas, whom was overwhelmed by the supernatural encounter, sat down and reflected closely on what was asked of him. Half an hour later Joseph awoke and took over the sailing duties once more.

"Joseph the Holy Spirit has contacted me whilst you were sleeping and has tasked me with the duty of publishing a letter for the people of Australia" Lucas exclaimed.

"Praise be to Heavenly Father, brother! What will the letter say?" Joseph exclaimed and asked.

"I don't know yet what is to be written in this letter, I will only know when I reach Benalla" Lucas said.

Lucas slumped down into the hull of the cruising yacht and laid out on the white couch. He drifted off reflecting over and over on the task and the place he was commanded to carry it out.

Chapter 8

It was Monday 6th February, 2017 when Lucas and Joseph finally docked in at Frances Bay in Darwin once again. Like their previous voyage through the Timor Sea they were intercepted only twice by Australian Patrol boats and neither inspection of the vessel came across Joseph's cache of firearms (minus the Stevens 555 shotgun Joseph had bestowed on Jacob).

Utilising a public internet Wi-Fi access at the McDonalds restaurant on Stuart Highway, which was a twenty minute walk from where they had docked, Lucas took to e-mailing Vincent.

> *Hi V,*
> *J and I have sailed back into Aus waters.*
> *Will be back in your neck of the woods in a couple of*
> *weeks.*
> *Will keep in touch.*
> *Regards,*
> *L*

Lucas also sent an encrypted e-mail to Jacob and Emily stating simply that they had "landed".

Keen to shake off their sea legs, Lucas and Joseph trekked half an hour up the road to Parap Village Markets to peruse the shops. When passing by the newsagency Lucas took to looking through the assorted newspapers to gauge what the system propaganda was dishing out to the public since they'd been gone.

Several of the headlines were strongly pressing for a war with Russia, characterising then Russian President Alexander Demushkin as the "Hitler of our time" and a "war criminal". These monikers had been bestowed on President Demushkin for having taken defensive military action against the CIA backed Russophobe right-wing death squads whom were officially under the military leadership of Ukrainian President Abraham Revusky.

This foreign policy situation was being capitalised on by ASIO to accelerate their manufactured mandate via the "inquiry into anti-system extremists" to beef up anti-terrorism legislation and systematically arrest key domestic proponents, pundits and activists for whiteness expansion.

ASIO's counterpropaganda funding towards Trades Hall tacticians had by this time evolved into tacit support for the roving mentally unstable street thug cadres whom had attacked Vincent in broad daylight without any further investigation. These same cadres, whom had become notorious for chanting "kill whitey" and "burn Nazi homes", had taken to posting glossy graphics savvy posters around the city invoking an innocuous camouflage campaign of "STOP WAR IN UKRAINE" and "SAY NO TO RACISM".

As the evening began to set-in Lucas and Joseph once again set sail, heading eastward towards the northern point of Queensland's coastline.

Meanwhile Jacob and Emily had commandeered the three rooms at the back of Luar Biasa Printing Pty Ltd, moving out of their residence at Villa Puri Royan motel. They figured why pay the motel fees when they had the ostensibly free lodgings and amenities provided to them by the Indonesian state intelligence agency.

Jacob whom was still continuing to work for the screen-printing business that was re-producing his 'Revolt Against The Synarchist Vampires' designs on t-shirts and tote bags, was able to steadily spread his time between both premises. Emily too was still maintaining her employment as a multitasking clairvoyant, yoga teaching, bar tendering, artist.

The spooks at Radio Free Encounter, which oversaw a newspaper, radio station and social media activist collective whose supporters wore bright orange shirts with the letter "E" emblazoned on them in black, were keen to make their watchful eyes known to both Jacob and Emily.

Radio Free Encounter supporters, known colloquially as the "orang oranye" (orange people), began routinely popping up around both Jacob and Emily's workplaces keeping tabs on their movements. Kadek had reminded Jacob and Emily that if these "orang oranye" political cultists were to make a violent move against them that Indonesian law permitted the use of certain firearms for self-defence.

By this time Vincent and Larissa had returned from their

stay around Eaglehawk at The Great Stupa of Universal
Compassion. Vincent, who made sure to keep his electronic
devices switched off for their meditation trip, had received
Lucas's email and responded accordingly.

> *G'day L,*
> *Glad to hear you fellas made it back without issue.*
> *Be great to catch up with you soon!*
> *Regards,*
> *V*

Vincent, who'd been fending off media calls to outright ban
'Stake Of Truth' magazine, was relieved to hear two of his
valued contributors were coming back to face the contempt
of blow-dried blowhards passing as "talking heads" for the
Operation Mockingbird controlled media.

Vincent's brother Tom had taken up the position of co-editor
of the magazine, along with Larissa and her sister Jessica.
All three of them had Bachelor of Communication degrees;
Tom having Majored in Public Relations, Larissa having
Majored in Creative Writing and Jessica having Majored in
Journalism. This enabled Vincent to focus more time on his
chiropractic practice and the other side businesses he had
going.

Meanwhile Lucas and Joseph were nearing Port Douglas in
Queensland once again for a stopover. Going ashore they
took a walk through the township and grabbed a table at the
Thai and seafood Star of Siam restaurant.

"Lucas we should dock back in at Coffs Harbour in about ten
days" Joseph said.

"When we dock I'll need to be heading down South to stay with my mate Caleb in Swan Hill" Lucas stated.

"Sure we can't take a day or two to get our bearings in Coffs Harbour?" Joseph asked.

"I can't, the Lord has tasked me with the publishing of this letter. I'll need to push on as was commanded of me" Lucas replied.

"No problems brother, I'll be there alongside you" Joseph assured.

Lucas and Jacob casually took their time eating and reacquainting themselves with the township for a couple of hours before they were to board the yacht once more. Whilst Joseph went to the Coles supermarket on Macrossan Street Lucas attended a heritage listed white weatherboard church called St Mary's by the Sea.

Lucas went inside and sat on the front row pew looking out the window behind the pulpit unto the ocean view which came right up to the back of the building. The sun shone brightly through the window amongst a bright blue sky filled with pure white clouds.

Reflecting again on the words having been spoken to him earlier that month by the hypnotic white flames above the ocean surface, Lucas contemplated why this letter writing task had been bestowed on him by God. He hardly was a sinless individual and hadn't attended church since growing up in Robinvale.

Lucas considered that God had chosen him much like the

Apostle Paul, whom had been a blasphemer and persecutor of Christians before being saved by grace through faith.

On the outer end of the pew lay a Bible that was opened to the first page of The Epistle of James. Lucas picked up the Bible and meditated on James 1:2-8 which read:

Consider it pure joy, my brothers and sisters, whenever you face trials of many kinds, because you know that the testing of your faith produces perseverance. Let perseverance finish its work so that you may be mature and complete, not lacking anything. If any of you lacks wisdom, you should ask God, who gives generously to all without finding fault, and it will be given to you. But when you ask, you must believe and not doubt, because the one who doubts is like a wave of the sea, blown and tossed by the wind. That person should not expect to receive anything from the Lord. Such a person is double-minded and unstable in all they do.

Lucas knelt on the wooden floor of the church and looked out the window at the sun as he prayed the following prayer out loud:

Dear God,

Please give me the wisdom and strength to not be tempted by doubt and unbelief in carrying out this mission you have commanded of me. Please also give me and my friends the necessary wisdom and strength to overcome the persecution being levelled against our contributions to alternative truth-seeking media.

I ask this in the name of Jesus. Amen.

As Lucas rose to stand he felt a crushing sense of certainty take hold of him in what he had to do. Although he was yet unsure what this letter was to communicate his conviction in writing it was cemented in place and he felt sure no temporal distraction could cause him to lose sight of what he was destined to do.

Lucas casually walked out of the church and made his way back to where the yacht was docked. Joseph was loading a couple of bags of groceries aboard when Lucas arrived.

"Ready to set sail brother?" Joseph asked.

"Absolutely!" Lucas replied.

Lucas and Joseph boarded and readied the yacht once more for their journey down the coast to Coffs Harbour.

Meanwhile anonymous tormenters had begun bombarding the area around Vincent's home and chiropractic practice with leaflets accusing him of being a "racist", "sexist", "fascist", "homophobe", "satanist" and "paranoid schizophrenic".

Tom thoroughly documented the flyer bombing campaign with a series of photos and on the ground remarks from residents and business owners who had come into contact with the propaganda. Vincent drafted an editorial for the March edition of Stake Of Truth magazine whereby he blamed the smear operation on paid riff-raff working on behalf of the Occult Operations Executive (OOE).

In fact the riff-raff whom Vincent was referring to were the same provocateurs larping as a "satanic Nazi paramilitary group" as characterised by the Sydney Afternoon Messenger. 'Van Helsing Division' was ostensibly little more than a two pronged shape-shifter outfit run by ASIO to both take the form of skull mask donning "Nazis" and black bloc "anti-fascists".

Whilst not all the persons that had been caught up in the milieu of this psychological operation were paid agitators, the tacticians that were leading the charge were in fact direct agents working for ASIO officers.

Jacob and Emily, who had been receiving reports via e-mail from Vincent about what was transpiring in Victoria, had taken to sketching up artwork that portrayed a romanticised effort on behalf of Stake Of Truth contributors to battle the corrupt tactics of the system.

Emily had taken to creating an artistic rendition of Vincent being portrayed as a modern day Martin Luther nailing his 95 theses on the door of Wittenberg Castle church. Lucas had sketched an image of Vincent brandishing a quill and writing the partial turn of phrase "mightier than the sword".

By this stage the "orang oranye" working for Radio Free Encounter were trying similar tactics against Jacob and Emily also. A cartoon strip in the Radio Free Encounter newspaper "Bali Dialogue" portrayed Jacob and Emily as foreign spies secretly soliciting "anti-Hindu" and "anti-Islam" propaganda.

However, there was sufficient counterpropaganda sponsored by the Indonesian state intelligence agency to let the general public in Bali know that Radio Free Encounter was "penipuan Yankee" (Yankee fraud).

Meanwhile on Wednesday 22nd February Lucas and Joseph had docked in at Coffs Harbour. Upon arriving Joseph took to a public payphone nearby the Marina to make a call to his father. Lucas too made a call to his friend Caleb.

"Caleb mate, how ya going?" Lucas asked as he filled up the phone with coins.

"Eh Lucas you nutter! Yeah things have been good as gold here. Whereabouts you hailing from at the minute?" Caleb asked.

"Up in Coffs Harbour at the minute. Wondering if a mate and I can come crash at your place for three nights?" Lucas asked.

"Yeah, no probs mate. I'll let the missus know you'll be bunkering down with us." Caleb said.

"Cheers mate! We should be at your joint around tomorrow afternoon" Lucas stated.

"Nice one, I'll see you then" Caleb responded.

Lucas hanged the phone up and made his way with Joseph to a nearby cafe for lunch. Joseph had organised with his father Graham to bring his Ford Falcon Ute down to the Marina car park so Lucas and he could load up their belongings direct from the yacht and carry on down to Swan Hill.

Lucas, who was using a power outlet in the back corner of the cafe to charge his laptop, had taken to using the public Wi-Fi to send an e-mail to his brother Jack letting him know they'd just got back into the country without any hassle.

By 3:00pm Graham had made his way to the Marina with Joseph's Ford Falcon Ute and the three of them loaded up the vehicle with their belongings and provisions leftover from the voyage. Graham and Joseph went for a walk to Eric & Deb's Homemade Ice Cream parlour to grab a milkshake each and then went for stroll along the Jetty Beach to catch up.

Lucas took to firing off an encrypted e-mail to Vincent and Jacob stating:

> *Hey guys,*
> *We've docked back in at J's hometown Marina.*
> *We're going to be getting on the road later.*
> *Will have an open letter ready to publish soon.*
> *Regards,*
> *L*

Lucas then went to make another call at the payphone to Geoff, whom Lucas had met some months prior at the National Electoral Committee (NEC) meeting.

"Hey Geoff, it's Lucas Leary here. We'd met each other last year at the NEC meeting in Coburg" Lucas outlined.

"Ah yeah, how's it going cobber? You still working in the city?" Geoff asked.

"Nah, been taken abroad for these last couple of months. A mate and I are heading down through Benalla in a couple days for a night or two. Was wondering if you were going to be at your property up there" Lucas stated suggestively.

"The family and I won't be up there till April, but if you guys are looking for a place to crash I'd be happy to loan you out the house for a small fee" Geoff offered.

"That'd be great! Whereabouts is the house?" Lucas asked.

"101 Faithfull street, Benalla. There's a spare key in a fake rock by the fence line left of the carport. Leave $100 on the dining table and promise to keep the place as you found it and you are welcome to stay" Geoff stated.

"Thanks Geoff, I owe you one! I'll be heading back down to the city after two nights. I'll give you a buzz when we're down" Lucas said gratefully.

"Sounds good Lucas, see you soon" Geoff stated.

Lucas hanged the phone up and made his way back over the road to the cafe to wait for Joseph and Graham to get back from their walk. Around 4:45pm Joseph returned, parting ways with Graham over a handshake and hug.

Lucas and Joseph then readied themselves for the fourteen and half hour trip to Swan Hill. As they pulled out of the car park at the Marina they loaded the CD player up with the 1976 album "Boston". As they hit the Pacific Highway they blasted the tune "Long Time" as they drove southward to their destination back in Victoria.

Chapter 9

Lucas was walking along a railway track somewhere in rural Australia. The sky above was an elaborate mixture of yellow, orange and red which complimented the fields of pasture Lucas passed as he tread in an unknown direction.

Lucas was walking towards a glimmering white light, although it was too distant to ascertain what was causing it's hypnotic illumination.

Alongside the railway tracks were trenches that were bursting with high grass and shrubs. As Lucas trekked forward he looked behind him to see the grass and shrubs igniting into blackened flames. From the flames emerged masked dark blue uniformed police wielding throwing spears.

As Lucas picked up pace the police mirrored his speed and threw their spears in Lucas's direction. The ground under Lucas's feet began to radiate with heat until it forced him unto the railway tracks which were cold as ice.

As Lucas ran with increasing speed he suddenly was
struck by a full body jolt that felt like an intense myoclonic
seizure. He then experienced a dimensional shift and was
all of sudden rapidly falling past an obliterated landscape of
twisted skyscraper frames. The ground below was transfixed
with the same mysterious white light from before.

As Lucas fell faster and faster the white light began to creep
like a vine around the steel beams and floors of cement that
surrounded him. Looking over his shoulder from where he
was falling was a sky filled with rainforest.

Looking back to the ground Lucas felt a radiating pulse
emanate from below. Just as he was about to hit the
illuminated white light with great force he was jolted awake
in the front seat of Joseph's Ford Falcon Ute.

Joseph had the CD player loaded up with the album
"Blizzard of Ozz" and the song "Crazy Train" was blasting
out the speakers. They were passing through Tarro by this
time and the two of them decided to stop for a break off the
road.

They drove into the BP Truckstop on Kinta Drive, Beresfield
at around 9:00pm and parked the ute. After utilizing the
bathroom facilities they ordered some burgers at the Hungry
Jack's restaurant that was on site and secured a booth to sit
and eat whilst they grabbed their bearings.

"I think we are still about eleven hours from reaching Caleb's
joint" Lucas said as he took a big bite out of the Whopper
burger he'd purchased.

"Might be worth grabbing some motel rooms near here for

the night" Joseph responded.

"There was a place we passed five minutes up the road. We'll double back to book in there" Lucas said in agreement.

After Lucas and Joseph had eaten they drove back up the highway to the Palm Valley Motel booking into two rooms adjacent to one another for the night.

Meanwhile Tom, Larissa and Jessica, who were spending the evening ironing out the editorial work for the March edition of the magazine, had factored in a four page spread layout for Lucas's open letter near the front of the next issue. Vincent, who was coordinating with the two graphic designers that worked on Stake Of Truth's typesetting and advertisement designs, was ironing out details pertaining to new advert orders featuring in the next quarterly issues.

The eclectic range of advertising clients who'd been flocking to Vincent's support base (despite the negative press from the establishment media) came primarily from small to medium sized businesses whose owners sympathised with those dubbed "conspiracy theorists" by the system.

Whilst some of these clients were beginning to be harassed by agitators who'd been targeting the publication it was generally the case that such persecution only reinforced their resilience and conviction in doing business with Vincent.

By midnight Vincent, Tom, Larissa and Jessica had stepped away from their various duties to partake of three bottles of Jacob's Creek Double Barrel Cabernet Sauvignon. Situating themselves out in the back pergola of Vincent and Larissa's Ivanhoe home they kicked back in good spirits.

"How we going with the March layout?" Vincent asked.

"Everything writing wise is mostly prepared for publication. Probably have the last of it finished by Friday." Tom outlined.

"Good to here! I'm hoping Lucas to have the letter over to us by Tuesday so we can get moving on the printing and shipping." Vincent stated.

"Do we know what the letter entails?" Jessica asked.

"Not as yet but given what he has been providing us previously I assume it's going to be good." Vincent said reassuringly.

"Vince, let's turn off talking about the magazine for a while" Larissa suggested.

"No problems, hun. Who is up for a game of trivia?" Vincent asked as he drank down the rest of his glass of wine.

By this time Jacob and Emily had also taken to a drinking session back in Bali. The Nazi-themed bar called "SoldatenKneipe" (aka The Soldiers' Bar) was a popular drinking spot were Emily had been picking up bar tending shifts over the last couple of months.

Frequently taking to exhibiting her large Black Sun symbol tattoo when posing for photos with customers who either had similar insignias tattooed on them and/or gestured the roman salute, Emily was a popular personality around the place.

Intoxicatingly making out as they ran their hands over one

another in a lounge area sectioned off by a beaded swastika curtain at the back end of the bar, Jacob and Emily laid themselves out on a leather couch whilst knocking back flaming shots of absinthe and Bintang beers.

Three of Emily's friends who were around that evening kept an eye on four conspicuous "orang oranye" who were intermittently perving on Jacob and Emily from the midsection of the bar. Jacob who had his .32 automatic colt pistol close at hand under the couch was just itching for one of these orange stalkers to give him a justification to fire off some shots.

"Babe I've got to take a piss. I'll be back in a tick." Jacob stated as he got up whilst kissing Emily on the neck and slipping the gun into her right hand.

"Okay, hun." Emily replied.

Jacob walked down the corridor at the other side of room which was plastered with WWII memorabilia. Turning left through the door into the men's bathroom, Jacob lit up a Djarum Black cigarette as he took aim at the urinal.

A couple of seconds later two of the "orang oranye" came blazing through the door behind him. One of them brandishing a syringe and the other grabbing Jacob in a bear hug as he told his offsider to "Menyuntikkan Jacob!" ("Inject Jacob!").

Before the two of them had a chance to dose Jacob up with the unknown contents of the syringe one of Emily's mates came in brandishing a pistol yelling "Jangan bergerak" ("Do not move"). The "orang oranye" with the syringe dropped it and the other one let go of Jacob. They both raised their hands and put their backs to the wall.

Jacob picked up the syringe and kneed one of the "orang oranye" in the gut. He motioned to Emily's mate to watch them and keep them there. Jacob burst through the bathroom door and made his way back to Emily.

"Babe give us the gun!" Jacob sternly stated as he stashed the syringe under a Waffen-SS Paratrooper helmet displayed on the mantelpiece.

Emily handed Jacob the .32 automatic colt pistol as he swiftly turned and made his way over to the two other "orang oranye" that had been watching them. Jacob pointed the gun at them and motioned for them to move in the direction of the bathroom. As one of the "orang oranye" attempted to dart for the front exit the other two of Emily's mates who'd been watching them intercepted and dragged him up the corridor.

Emily closely followed behind them as they all flowed back into the bathroom. As the four "orang oranye" were lined up against the bathroom wall together, one of Emily's mates interrogated them in Balinese as another translated to Jacob what they confessed.

Emily took out her mobile and phoned Kadek, their contact in the Indonesian state intelligence agency.

"Kadek we've had the oranges try to jab Jacob, we're squeezing them for information at the moment" Emily cryptically stated as Kadek answered the phone.

"Take mugshots of them and text them through to me" Kadek

replied.

"Ok, what do we do with them?" Emily asked.

"Keep them there, I'll have my POLRI contacts pick them up soon" Kadek directed as he ended the call.

Emily snapped photos of the four "orang oranye" and messaged them to Kadek as her three mates corralled them out the bathroom and down the corridor. They bunkered down in a room off to the right decked out with a roundtable emblazoned with a swastika and walls covered in framed photos of Adolf Hitler.

As the "orang oranye" were seated down at the table two of Emily's mates stationed themselves at the entranceway with guns in hand. The third went to wait front of house to direct Kadek's contacts in the National Police (POLRI) to where they were held up out back. Jacob and Emily lit up a Djarum Black cigarette each and took a seat by the right wall of the room.

It was just under an hour later when six officers entered the bar and were brought out back to arrest the four "orang oranye". The officers handcuffed them and pressed Detachment 88 issued SIG MPX submachine guns into their backs as they pushed the prisoners past patrons back out to the street where a paddy wagon awaited them.

As they POLRI officers drove away Jacob and Emily casually exited the bar and caught a Bluebird taxi back to Luar Biasa Printing Pty Ltd, where they bunkered down for what remained of the night.

The next morning Lucas and Joseph got up around 6:00am to hit the road once more for their destination in Victoria. They commuted back to the Hungry Jacks they'd previously dined at some hours earlier and grabbed themselves a hot drive-thru breakfast.

As Joseph drove down the highway Lucas loaded the CD player up with the song "Uprising" by Muse. The song blared out the speakers of the car as Lucas and Joseph nonchalantly sung along in and out of tune. By the time they drove into Wagga Wagga for a cuppa and pit stop the atmosphere in the car had come to an energetic crescendo with "Jumpin' Jack Flash" by The Rolling Stones playing loudly.

After they departed Wagga Wagga Lucas dozed off to the tune of "Teardrop" by Massive Attack.

A wave of overwhelming white light transported Lucas before a court room which dispersed the light like a hand being raised to shield one's eyes from the sun. Standing beside Lucas in the defendant dock was the cherub Mebahel who wore a grey suit, black shirt and white tie.

Seated in the judge's seat was the seraphim Sitael who wore a black robe before a raised judicial bench that bore the biblical verse Revelations 6:8...

"And I looked, and behold a pale horse: and his name that sat on him was Death, and Hell followed with him. And power was given unto them over the fourth part of the earth, to kill with sword, and with hunger, and with death, and with the beasts of the earth."

Seated at the plaintiff's table was the angel Mumiah who

wore a green suit, yellow shirt and red bow tie. Mumiah wielded a briefcase that when opened revealed a trove of gum leaves. Mumiah ignited the gum leaves and presented a statement before judge Sitael as smoke surrounded him with a mystical veneer.

"Your Honour,

The madness of this man knows much of what is unseen yet lacks the hope to heal his people from the scourge of darkness. He seeks the end of the wicked blood sucking, currency collapsing, disease spreading, queer enabling, child corrupting, usurious, nation destroyers but would sell his soul to do so.

I request this high time preference psycho be put to an end and reborn as a shaman traversing the trance of transfiguration."

Mebahel then produced a slender bamboo needled tool to perform a tebori tattoo on Lucas's Right hand of a Celtic cross.

"We're here mate" Joseph said as he nudged Lucas awake.

As the two fellas got out of their car Caleb came walking out the front door to greet them.

"Hey Leary, how are ya'?" Caleb called out light heartedly.

"Could be better with a shot of whisky mate!" Lucas replied.

"Caleb, this is my mate Joseph" Lucas stated as he introduced the two.

"Come in fellas will get you sorted with something to eat and drink."

As Lucas and Joseph gathered up their belongings and made their way inside the three of them sat down to catch up.

Whilst Lucas and Caleb toasted with whiskey Joseph as per usual toasted with water.

Chapter 10

Over the next three days Lucas, Joseph and Caleb loitered around Caleb's skater shop playing pool and chin-wagging about all that had transpired since Lucas and Caleb had last seen each other.

Caleb was engrossed in Lucas' colourful retelling of working off the side of sky-scrapers in Melbourne, relocating to Coffs Harbour, the fall of Rek-Wiz-It magazine, the rise of Stake Of Truth magazine, the false flag assassination attempt of Dr. Jonathan Foxman and the process of evading the ASIO dragnet by sailing to Bali to run counterpropaganda operations in ostensible exile.

On the second day people who Lucas knew around town had stopped by for a booze up out back, with fifty odd punters celebrating Lucas' return from early afternoon to around midnight.

The following day, Sunday 26th February (the final day of staying at Caleb's place), Lucas used the business Wi-

Fi to e-mail Vincent and NEC organizer Vanessa about the explosive letter he was set to have ready to be submitted for publication in a matter of hours.

When they were ready to depart Caleb's place by late morning, Lucas being unsure of what would transpire after this letter went to print, took to imparting his unpublished writing journals to Caleb for safe keeping.

"Mate do me a favour and hold on to these for me" Lucas said to Caleb.

"Sure thing Leary! When you going to be back up this way?" Caleb asked.

"God only knows mate. Hopefully sooner rather than later." Lucas replied.

As Lucas and Caleb made parting chit-chat, and giving one another a quick bro hug, Joseph finished loading the bags in the ute. As Lucas and Joseph started to drive off Joseph gave two toots of the vehicle horn, waved out the window and drove off in the direction of Benalla.

By this time Jacob and Emily had been called up by Kadek to meet at Ngurah Rai International Airport with their luggage. Kadek greeted them by providing two pre-paid tickets to return back to Australia that afternoon.

"I recommend returning to Australia. These dupes of the CIA who targeted you the other day have connections with organized crime syndicates in our country. These dogs will sooner bite first and not ask questions later" Kadek stated to Jacob and Emily.

"What about the Australian security services? Will they likely be taking an interest in us coming back in?" Jacob asked.

"I'm sure the Americans will have forwarded intel to your government's security services. My recommendation is refrain from telling them anything when you land. I will have my people go through your belongings to ensure there is nothing that ASIO can use as incriminating evidence and we will provide you with paperwork that will prove exculpatory regarding your presence here in Bali" Kadek replied.

Jacob and Emily spent the day at the airport going through a security debriefing with Kadek's agents and they boarded a flight around 2:00pm that day. When they landed in Melbourne around 8:00pm they were met with close scrutiny by customs and three Australian Federal Police (AFP) officers, however were released some hours later without charge.

Lucas and Joseph had arrived at the four bedroom red brick house at 101 Faithfull street, Benalla late that afternoon and had swiftly taken to setting themselves up for the night.

As Lucas set-up a writing space in the front room of the house, Joseph noted that they would need some provisions for their brief stay.

"Lucas I'm going to Woolworths to get some food, did you want anything in particular for dinner" Joseph asked.

"I'm easy mate, grab whatever you reckon" Lucas replied.

As Joseph exited the front door, took to the ute once more

and backed out of the driveway Lucas kicked backed in front of his writing space and enjoyed the silence of his own company.

Over the course of the next forty-five minutes Lucas typed away at his laptop at lightning speed in a somewhat trance like state. Lucas' inspired letter numbered some four thousand words by the time Joseph returned.

As Joseph pieced together a meal of roast chicken, coleslaw and Greek salad for the two of them Lucas emailed off the letter to Vincent with the following message:

> *Dear V,*
>
> *Here are the inspired words imparted on me from that vast and hitherto unknown realm half an inch back of our foreheads (Terra Incognita).*
>
> *Stay safe brother!*
>
> *Regards,*
>
> *L*

Lucas and Joseph proceeded to eat dinner together over casual conversation when all of a sudden there was a knock at the door. As it was now dark outside the two compatriots looked at one another with puzzled expression.

Joseph took to the door whilst Lucas peered through the curtains out the front window at the doorstep to see who was knocking.

"Joseph wait!" Lucas whispered emphatically.

Lucas could make out two plain clothed persons wearing sidearms accompanied by six uniformed police officers. On the street was parked a black vehicle, four divvy vans with lights flashing and media camera crews stationed over the opposite side of the street.

The knocking continued to get louder. Lucas quickly stuffed his laptop into his carry bag and darted for the back door.

"Joseph out the back!" Lucas once again emphatically whispered.

As Lucas exited through the back wire door two uniformed officers tackled him to the ground.

"Mate relax! Stay down! You're under arrest!" one of the uniformed officers sternly stated to Lucas as the two officers forced Lucas' hands behind his back and handcuffed him.

Lucas could hear Joseph at the front of the property talking to the officers but couldn't quite make out what was being said.

The two officers that had nabbed Lucas around the back of the property escorted Lucas around the side of the house and out to the street where prying cameras were eagerly waiting to get the footage of the elusive Earl Pierce.

As Lucas' hands were cuffed behind his back, so he couldn't cover his face with his hands, and the police hadn't done anything to conceal his face from public view, Lucas was keenly aware this was an ostensible perp walk for the media.

Lucas had his laptop taken and was swiftly loaded into the back of one of the divvy vans, but not before seeing that police had gained access through the front door.

As the divvy van door was shut and locked Lucas sat in silence and took in the dark surround of the cramped stuffy space he occupied. Lucas mentally stamped out doubt in his mind that the system had yet won.

Meanwhile Vincent had received the letter and was promptly editing it, which Vincent swiftly and surprisingly found was absent of spelling or grammatical errors. About three quarters of an hour later, as Vincent finished proof reading through the letter, he mass sent copies of it in PDF form to his list of a dozen odd hardcopy and digital publications who would help to disseminate what was going on at Stake Of Truth magazine.

As the email was sent knocks at the front door of Vincent's Ivanhoe home sounded throughout the house. Vincent answered the door to find a similar scene as to what had transpired a couple of hours earlier that evening in Benalla.

"Vincent Tynan we have a warrant to search your property, please come with us" stated a plain clothed female officer.

"I'd like to phone my lawyer first" Vincent promptly responded

"You'll be able to ring your lawyer when we get you to the station. At this present moment you're under arrest for the offense of sedition under section 80.2A(1)(c) of the Criminal Code Act 1995" responded the female officer.

Police then proceeded to handcuff Vincent and escort him to
a black BMW X5.

Jacob and Emily by this time were holding out at the two-
bedroom property Jacob's uncle owned in Broadmeadows.

They were watching television in bed when the breaking
story about Lucas' arrest was broadcasted:

*"In breaking news a joint operation between Victoria Police
and the Australian Federal Police has executed two arrests
tonight relating to the elusive far-right propagandist known
as 'Earl Pierce'. Channel 6 News has been informed that the
identity of 'Earl Pierce' is a male in his mid-twenties named
Lucas Leary. At the present moment Mr. Leary has been taken
in for questioning."*

"Fuck!" Jacob said despairingly.

"What should we do?" Emily asked.

"I don't know but the AFP didn't take us in this afternoon"
Jacob replied.

Jacob got up out of bed and walked into the living room. He
peered through the curtains of the front window, taking a seat
in the recliner by the wall nearest the front door and picked
up the television remote to scroll through the channels.

Emily took to the kitchen and turned on the electric kettle to
make her and Jacob a cup coffee. The talking points from the
24-hour news cycle emanated throughout the house.

Lucas by this time was being processed with a psych

assessment at the police station in Benalla. Prying questions about Lucas' psychiatric history, medical history, family history, social history and substance use and abuse by a forensic psychologist were met with cryptic and abstract responses.

When the psychologist had finished with his questions the two plain clothed officers that had attended the 101 Faithfull street residence some hours earlier directed Lucas to an adjacent interview room.

Lucas, who had been nursing a styrofoam cup of water, looked around the plain off colour white room whilst drumming his left-hand on the table in front of him. The two officers sat across from Lucas with their folders full of copies of evidence substantiating 'Revolt Against The Synarchist Vampires' as an ostensible "extremist" manifesto.

"Lucas my name is Inspector Belinda Wilson and this is my colleague Sergeant Joel Tynan. We're going to be recording this interview with the equipment to your left. You will need to refrain from banging your fingers on the table so as to not interfere with the microphone in front of you" Inspector Wilson stated.

"Just to be clear I am going to be giving a no comment interview" Lucas responded.

"That's entirely your choice Lucas but we will still proceed with our line of questioning" Inspector Wilson replied.

As Lucas affirmed initial questions pertaining to his name and lack of an address the officers proceeded to ask the following questions:

"Lucas you've written for either Rek-Wiz-It magazine or
Stake Of Truth magazine, yes?" asked Inspector Wilson.

"No comment" replied Lucas.

"Are you familiar with the serialised written piece in
these magazines entitled 'Revolt Against The Synarchist
Vampires'?" asked Inspector Wilson.

"No comment" replied Lucas.

"Have you ever gone by the alias 'Earl Pierce'?" asked
Sergeant Tynan.

"No comment" replied Lucas.

"We've been made aware that you have recently visited
Bali and yet there is no record of you having legally left the
country. We have it on good authority that you have been in
communication with an agent of the Badan Intelijen Negara.
Do you care to elaborate about this?" Inspector Wilson asked
in redirecting the line of questioning.

"No comment" replied Lucas.

Lucas, whilst not focusing on what was being asked,
continued to answer the questions with the same two-word
response.

Upon finishing the interrogation Lucas was placed back in a
room with the psych who'd being prying into his background
when first being brought into the station. It took the psych a
matter of forty-five minutes to decide that a recommendation

for a compulsory treatment order be applied for with the
Mental Health Tribunal.

Lucas was detained in a cell at the police station for the
next twelve hours until the compulsory treatment order
was approved. At 11:30am Monday 27th February Lucas
was transferred to a secure forensic mental health hospital
to be injected with depot antipsychotics and placed under
observation.

By this time Vincent had been released by the police thanks
to the assistance of his lawyer Mark Jameson.

Vincent had been issued a cease and desist letter by police
over Stake Of Truth magazine being continued to be
published whilst their investigation was ongoing. Stake Of
Truth's short-lived existence appeared to have hit a similar
fate as that which was levelled against Rek-Wiz-It magazine.

Jacob had sent Vincent an encrypted e-mail which read:

> *V,*
>
> *Hi mate, E and I are stationed where L was bunkered
> down before leaving Vic.*
> *Cops have arrested L.*
> *No word as to what happened to his mate J.*
> *Let me know when you're okay to talk.*
>
> *Regards,*
>
> *J*

Vincent replied by writing:

Hi J,

Just been released by the cops.
Meet me tomorrow at Va Tutto 2:00pm

Regards,

V

Vincent queried why it was that nothing had yet filtered through about what had befell Joseph.

Where was Joseph?

Chapter 11

"The target had spent much of his time in Bali dining in district eateries, drinking and using psychedelics whilst cooperating with the Badan Intelijen Negara. The target was routinely prone to bouts of delusions of grandeur and psychotic breaks with reality in which he believed a transnational system cabal was out to get him and exterminate large sways of the global population." Joseph communicated to Inspector Belinda Wilson.

"Agent Pratt do you believe the target was of sound mind during your time spent observing him over the last number of months?" Inspector Wilson asked Joseph.

"I believe prosecuting Lucas Leary as being of sound mind would be a catastrophic course of action for our agencies to pursue!" Joseph emphatically replied.

"For the record can you please expand on this?" Inspector Wilson prompted Joseph.

"Whilst he is ostensibly a skilled autodidactic writer who is both high functioning and deeply paranoid, his readers are likely just as obsessed and paranoid as he is. If we were to lend credence to the notion that Mr. Leary's conspiratorial hypergraphia writings were anything more than delusional rants we ostensibly validate his self-fulfilling prophecy of a martyr and political prisoner against the system." Joseph outlined to Inspector Wilson.

Joseph Pratt had been an operative of ASIO for some years. His life in the Church of Jesus Christ of Latter-day Saints had primed him as an asset for the agency, as he'd learnt a second language in preparation for his two-year service when carrying out a mission for the church.

ASIO had initially identified Joseph as a prime recruit based upon his father Graham Pratt having served the majority of his army service in military intelligence and who was also a committed Freemason.

The Pratt's focus on discourses from the milieu of conservative, right-wing, reactionary and conspiratorial politics pertained mainly to their goal of identifying conduits of influence who were "counter-intentional" towards the goals of the system.

The articles which Joseph had submitted to Rek-Wiz-It and Stake Of Truth magazines under the alias 'Hyrum Young' had in fact been penned by the Occult Operations Executive (OOE) whom had overseen the 'Van Helsing Division' operation.

Joseph Pratt had been working to secure sufficient evidence

to bring Lucas under control and implode the publishing operations of Vincent.

Meanwhile Vincent and Jacob had met up at Va Tutto restaurant in Ivanhoe.

"Mate I'm stuffed if I know how Lucas got found out" Jacob stated stupefyingly to Vincent.

"Our emails have been encrypted so I'm doubtful they have been tracking our movements that way. Maybe they caught them on CCTV somewhere when coming back in Australia?" Vincent asked.

"Maybe. I wonder why we haven't heard anything about Joseph though?" Jacob asked.

"Don't know but until we find out what is going on with Lucas just assume eyes are on us" Vincent replied.

"What about Lucas' letter?" Jacob asked.

"Stake Of Truth won't be able to publish with this bullshit cease and desist letter from the feds but our publishing allies will hopefully syndicate it" Vincent replied.

By this stage Lucas, who was under the effect of powerful chemical straightjacket drugs, was being probed by a psychiatrist.

"Lucas my name is Dr. Jasmine Levy. Do you understand why you are here?" Dr. Levy asked Lucas.

"I understand that it's easier to write me off as a lone nut than a prophetic voice against the system you serve" Lucas replied in a muttering tone.

"Can you explain to me what you think this system is that you invoke?" Dr. Levy asked further.

"It's a multifaceted exterminationist pyramid of parasitism, plutocracy and persecution" Lucas stated frustratingly to Dr. Levy.

"Lucas how do you feel at the moment?" Dr. Levy inquired further.

"What's that got to do with the price of tea in China?" Lucas said with a shrug.

"Lucas my job is to evaluate your mental health. If you could let me know how you're feeling it will assist me in determining the best course of action in helping you." Dr. Levy stated in an empathetic tone.

"Help? Would a transorbital lobotomy be defined as help, Dr. Levy?" Lucas asked sarcastically.

"Lucas those sorts of practices have long been relegated to the history books. We don't perform those sorts of procedures anymore!" Dr. Levy stated.

"As far as I'm concerned you're no different to Sidney Gottlieb and Louis Jolyon West. You are here to suppress me!" Lucas emphatically stated.

"Okay Lucas, we'll leave the conversation there for the moment. Is there anything I can do for you at present?" Dr.

Levy asked.

"Let me go" Lucas replied with a hint of jest.

Dr. Levy, upon leaving the consultation room with Lucas, proceeded to fill out an application form for a course of electroconvulsive therapy with the Mental Health Tribunal. Lucas would soon be inflicted with electrically induced generalized seizures for having spoken against the system.

Lucas was escorted back to his room and began to read a book called "Be the best you" by Dr. Ronald Gresham which ostensibly was filled with inoffensive validating platitudes and psychobabble mixed with trite truisms.

Meanwhile Vanessa had been one of the dozen or so contacts who'd received Vincent's encrypted mass e-mail with Lucas' letter attached and had taken to formatting it in the upcoming issue of 'The Neo National'. Similarly, a half dozen other reactionary and right-wing bi-weekly papers and eight monthly magazines had the letter set for their next respective issues.

With the name 'Earl Pierce' echoing throughout the mainstream media the letter was deemed newsworthy by the revolutionary nationalist press.

It was by Thursday morning that the talking heads in the 24-hour news cycle started mentioning that Lucas had been committed to a secure forensic mental health hospital in Melbourne. The scripted press release, which was identically delivered by all major news presenters across free to air channels, read as such:

The press release, which was clearly designed to further
diminish the reputation of Lucas amongst the various
diversified publics in Australia, was mirrored in the Sydney
Afternoon Messenger, The Epoch and the Herald Star.

Vincent had meanwhile been communicating with Kole
Kramer, a colleague of his lawyer Mark Jameson who
specialised in appealing compulsory mental health treatment
orders.

"I'll be frank with you Mr. Tynan, Lucas Leary has got

himself a lot of publicity for all the wrong reasons." Kole stated to Vincent.

"Okay, but what are the chances of getting him released from the psych ward?" Vincent asked.

"Slim to none at the moment. The best bet we're going to have in seeing him released is a simultaneous relief in the public opinion, which the mainstream media is polluting, with an exculpatory subjective determination by his treating psychiatrist that he is of sound mind. At present though they seem to want this guy locked away for the things he writes and if they can do so whilst making him appear unstable to the public then all the better." Kole outlined to Vincent.

"I'd feel much better if we can at the very least start an appeal on his committal" Vincent stated.

"Leave it with me I'll see what I can do" Kole replied as he showed Vincent the door.

Over the next week as Kole made a submission of appeal to revoke the compulsory mental health treatment order against Lucas, the latest issue of 'The Neo National' was being disseminated on street corners throughout Melbourne, Sydney, Adelaide and Brisbane.

When the Socialist Association became aware that Lucas' letter had been featured on the front page of the paper street skirmishes broke out, particularly in Melbourne where the Socialist Association's main bulwark of career protestor support and leftist sympathizing government officials presided.

Naturally the skirmishes were honed in on by the system's mainstream media cartels and it wasn't the black bloc Socialist Association street criminals who were being maligned. One headline from the Sydney Afternoon Messenger read "Far-Right Extremists Attack Anti-Hate System Supporters".

A copy of the letter had also been leaked on several high traffic political forums online and some people had taken to IRL action by stencil graffitiing the words 'FREE EARL PIERCE' across public hotspots in municipalities around the country.

The various allied dissident print magazines started filtering out Lucas' letter by the second week of March with accompanying introductory articles. By the end of that week several fire bombings had taken place at mainstream media and governmental offices in regional, urban and metropolitan areas.

Meanwhile Lucas had gone through six sessions of electroconvulsive therapy following Dr. Jasmine Levy's application to the Mental Health Tribunal.

Lucas, who had elicited the goings-on beyond his clinical confines from psychiatric orderlies, was relishing in the upheaval that was transpiring from the letter commanded of him from white flames burning above the surface in the Timor Sea.

Whilst Lucas noted that since being committed to the psych ward he wasn't having the same visions or lucid dreams, since receiving forcible antipsychotic injections and electroshocks, he was reluctant in his communication with

Dr. Jasmine Levy.

"Lucas do you feel depressed?" Dr. Levy asked.

"Define depressed" Lucas stated.

"A sense of unhappiness" Dr. Levy responded.

"Well would you feel happy being stuck in here, Dr. Levy?" Lucas asked.

"Well do you recall how you were feeling before the police arrested you?" Dr. Levy further inquired.

"I felt anxious but I was free" Lucas replied.

"Why do you think you felt anxious, Lucas?" Dr. Levy asked.

"Because I know what the system is and knowing is my cross to carry" Lucas replied.

All of a sudden the session was stopped by a knock at the door.

"Dr. Levy we've got an urgent call for you on line three" a nurse said as she peered around door of the consultation room.

"Lucas we'll leave it there for the moment and pick this up again this afternoon" Dr. Levy stated.

"Sure" Lucas apathetically replied.

Lucas was shuffled out of the room by two black orderlies back to the common area in ward D.

The common area, a minimalist setting consisting of bolted down chairs and tables with a television behind secured reinforced laminated glass, housed patients during the day to prevent them from sleeping long periods in their rooms.

Products of the high carbohydrate diets and antipsychotic medications, the patients largely consisted of wretched overweight rambling zombies with an inability to remain still, a condition which the nurses referred to as "akathisia".

A court yard situated in the center of the building, accessed by a key pad and swipe card, was utilized by patients who smoked as a watching psychiatric orderly supervised.

Lucas had been denied access to newspapers under the psychiatric auspices of "health hazards". Apparently, according to Dr. Levy, the media coverage would fuel Lucas' "delusions" and exasperate his "pathological paranoia".

For the moment Lucas' reading resources were restricted to banal books that lacked anything that could be classified as politically or spiritually stimulating. Lucas was of the opinion that whilst he wasn't crazy upon arriving at this secure forensic psychiatric hospital the milieu control in here was literally driving him within an inch of his sanity.

In an attempt to take his mind off the annoying neurological nerfing present in the ward, Lucas opted to gain access to the court yard and walk laps.

As Lucas walked silently praying for a vision or sign

that would break him free of his predicament a bulky
schizophrenic aboriginal patient loitering in the center of the
courtyard who was talking to himself began to eyeballing
Lucas as he circled him.

All of sudden the patient launched himself in the direction
of Lucas brandishing a toothbrush, which the patient had
sharpened the handle of into a makeshift weapon.

"Fucking White dog!" the patient yelled.

Lucas swung around in time to react just as the aboriginal
patient plunged the sharpened toothbrush into the right side
of Lucas' chest. Lucas kicked the patient in the knee and
punched him in the throat. As the patient went to the ground,
grimacing in pain, Lucas applied pressure to the bloodied
area where the protruding toothbrush had been inflicted upon
him and rested up alongside the interior wall of the building.

Four orderlies came running over from the entrance side
of the yard to secure both Lucas and the aboriginal patient
away from one another. Lucas could taste blood pooling in
his mouth as he was escorted back into the main building and
down the corridor to the infirmary.

As Lucas was dragged towards the direction of a hospital bed
he saw flaring black flames engulf the room and his legs gave
out from underneath him.

Chapter 12

On April 19th 2018 a hearing was commenced before the Federal Court of Australia in Melbourne regarding the indictable charge put against Vincent for sedition. The proceedings carried on for a number of weeks and concluded with Mark Jameson making the following remarks in his closing statement to the court:

"Ladies and gentlemen of the jury, my client Vincent Tynan is an upstanding member of his community. He is the owner and operator of multiple successful businesses and is both a man of faith and conviction. Vincent and his family have been violently attacked by masked black bloc agitators, having had their home targeted multiple times with Molotov cocktails and his person assaulted in broad daylight by these cretinous criminals. The government authorities who have brought this case of sedition against my client have done little to nothing in investigating these overt crimes against him.

Instead what the government tenuously alleges is that my

*client's magazines, which has been syndicated in stores
up and down the East coast of Australia, are somehow an
'existential threat' to the democratic values of our society.*

*Let me just say I personally have differing political, social
and religious views to that of my client. However, I respect
his individual rights to express his freedom of thought,
speech and religion in the press he personally has willed into
existence by his blood and sweat.*

*My client, nor none of his staff of writers, have been shown
to have committed libel against any of the communities the
federal police have claimed they are "protecting" with this
laughable claim of sedition.*

*My client has published the demonstrably objective truth
and that is why the government authorities have pursued him
criminally rather than civilly.*

*A popular truism posited by George Orwell aptly states "In a
time of deceit telling the truth is a revolutionary act."*

*Ladies and gentlemen of the jury I ask you to decide; do
you side with those whose violence is considered "speech"
by the system or do you side with my client whose speech is
considered "violence" by the system?*

Whilst the deliberations of the jury took a day or so to come
back before the court it was a unanimous vindicating verdict
of 'not guilty' that reaffirmed Vincent's faith that the system
was yet to wield total control.

Within a day of the verdict, and over a year after Stake Of
Truth magazine had been issued a cease and desist letter by

Australian Federal Police, Vincent returned to publishing
the second stage of the magazine with a cover headline that
simply read 'Truth Triumphs'.

Jacob and Emily, who'd a couple months prior collaborated
on a water colour caricature portrait of Lucas, had Vincent set
it on the facing page of the feature article which took up five
pages of the next issue.

Lucas by this stage was still in the confines of Victoria's
psychiatric system.

Multiple applications by Kole Kramer to revoke Lucas'
compulsory treatment order had fallen on deaf ears with the
department of health, even despite continuing sporadic calls
for his release throughout Australia.

However, by this stage Dr. Jasmine Levy had authorized
Lucas to be given access to certain reading materials, which
he'd initially been prohibited from reading, and supplied
a writing pad and pen to jot down his thoughts. Lucas had
shifted from forcibly taking high dose injectable depot
antipsychotics to complying with daily scheduled pills being
dished out.

Lucas had reluctantly put on 26kg, weighing in at a
whopping 120kg, and the epiphanous clarity which Lucas
had wielded on the outside had been lost in a fog of
psychotropic narcotisation.

The electroconvulsive therapy had been applied on and off
over the last twelve months and it hadn't been until recently
that Lucas' brother Jack and sisters Sandra and Elise had
been allowed to visit him.

Correspondence from Vincent and Jacob to Lucas had been halted and the true identity of Joseph as an ASIO agent had filtered out in Vincent's trial.

"Lucas, what are your goals at the moment" Dr. Levy asked.

"I want to be released from this place!" Lucas replied.

"I see over the last year you've been involved in multiple violent altercations in our facility, yes?" Dr. Levy asked.

"You'll also see I was never the one initiating the violence" Lucas clarified.

"What does 'reckless' mean to you, Lucas?" Dr. Levy asked.

"A compulsion to self-destructiveness" Lucas replied.

"Would you characterise your previous activities before coming here as being 'reckless', Lucas?" Dr. Levy asked.

Lucas began rubbing his neck as he bent forward in the chair. He knew that unless he played along with the psych's pre-determined narrative he was never going to get out of this place.

"I suppose 'reckless' would be an apt characterisation" Lucas lamented.

"I think we've made progress Lucas. We'll take this up again tomorrow, in the meantime keep writing in you journal and we'll start looking at a mental health plan that will reconnect you back with the community" Dr. Levy said.

It was accurate to say Lucas was less alive than he was when he'd first entered the secure forensic mental health hospital. The defiance that stirred in him had been suppressed and life in the land of the loons had caused him to internalize some maddening habits.

As Lucas lit up a smoke in the low security court-yard he looked up at the sky watching a plane flying overhead. He thought to himself how long it would be before he could just get away from where he was.

He dropped his cigarette butt in the metal disposal unit by the door and had the orderly swipe him back in to the ward. He walked over to the administration desk and requested a newspaper from one of the psych nurses.

Lucas went and sat down at one of the tables and began flipping through the paper, eyeballing for a story that caught his interest. All of a sudden he froze on page eight when he read the headline 'ALA Chairman Receives Companion of the Order of Australia'.

> *"Dr. Jonathan Foxman, the Chairman of the Anti-Libel Alliance, has been awarded the Companion of the Order of Australia relating to his outstanding work at diligently fighting hate, extremism and terrorism. In November, 2016 Dr. Foxman was the target of an assassination attempt by a supporter of the far-right propagandist Lucas Leary, who has since been committed to a forensic psychiatric hospital following first-hand surveillance reports from the Australian Security Intelligence Organisation (ASIO)...*

Lucas repressed the urge to give the observing psychiatric staff in his vicinity any ammunition to write him up for a seemingly 'aberrant' outburst to the article. Glancing through the remaining pages of the paper, Lucas folded it back up and returned it back to the administration desk.

As much as Lucas wanted to write down how much of a bloodsucking sack of garbage he thought Dr. Foxman was, he knew communicating that in his journal would only stifle the possibility of him being released.

The initial flare-up that had eventuated after the publishing of Lucas' letter had petered out due to tabloid exploits misdirecting public focus. Fantastical system approved narratives and false-flags were repeatedly published as periodic reports of Lucas' deteriorating mental and physical health were lampooned.

Lucas had ostensibly come to represent the lost left-hand goat of the system, whilst the sheep on the right served the system blindly.

The following day when Lucas returned into session with Dr. Levy he presented an outward calmness so as to not derail his discharge prospects.

"So Dr. Levy you were saying last time that we could start working on my mental health plan and get me back into the community?" Lucas asked.

"Lucas what we need to discern is whether or not you are likely to revert back to the behaviors that got you here in the first place" Dr. Levy responded as she poured Lucas a glass of water.

"I can assure you I'm going to refrain from falling back into old habits" Lucas replied as he gulped down half the contents of the glass.

"What we'll do today Lucas are some psychological tests, does that sound okay with you?" Dr. Levy asked.

"Sure!" Lucas responded enthusiastically.

"They'll take about 45 minutes to an hour to complete so let's get started" Dr. Levy said with a smile.

Dr. Levy proceeded to ask Lucas a list of questions from a prepared series of papers. After twenty minutes or so Lucas began to feel strange. His heart beat seemed to increase whilst pulsating light and colour distortions overwhelmed the room. His vision began to get blurry, he began to sweat and his mouth became dry.

"Dr. Levy I…I…don't feel too…." Lucas stammered as he attempted to stand falling to the floor.

Lucas could see Dr. Levy's feet slowly walk around the table. She kneeled down beside him as the light in the room pulsated in sync with Lucas' heartbeat. When Lucas looked up at Dr. Levy's face it became distorted in an almost demonic looking fashion.

"What's the matter Mr. Pierce?" Dr. Levy's voice echoing in Lucas' ears.

"Why did you call me that?" Lucas asked as he drifted into a frenzied kaleidoscope of mental and physical overload.

Lucas found himself standing upon white sand cast against an ocean of blackness. The sky glimmered like an opal-coloured iris and every time Lucas blinked the waves crashed against his feet. Lucas looked off into the distance of the black ocean and saw white flames illuminating the horizon. As Lucas turned to view behind him inland, across the white sanded landscape, Lucas saw thousands of black headstones donned with Celtic crosses.

As Lucas walked up upon one of these headstones the white sand quickly swallowed Lucas' feet into a red muddied quicksand. He descended into a fall towards a blue marshmallow like surface as blobs of red and white fell alongside him.

Winds of yellow dust were seen skirting the blue surface as Lucas fell faster and faster. As Lucas impacted with the surface he once more broke through another surface and was now ascending through a green and orange cast of jelly.

As Lucas climbed the gelatine surrounds began to firm into sandstone like surfaces and when reaching the top Lucas laid down on the ground staring up at the flaming white sky.

Lucas stared until the sky once again morphed into the ceiling of the psych ward. Lucas tried to stand up but was unable to do so. He had been strapped into a five-point restraint in a seclusion room. Lucas began yelling.

After a couple minutes Lucas gave up and closed his eyes. Half an hour later Dr. Levy entered the room. She circled the restraint bed tapping a pen against her cheek.

"So Mr. Pierce how are you feeling?" Dr. Levy asked.

"My name is Lucas, Dr. Levy!" Lucas replied.

"Is it, Mr. Pierce?" Dr. Levy asked.

"Earl Pierce was an alias you want me to forget!" Lucas replied.

Dr. Levy began writing something in her folder whilst looking over her thick rimmed glasses.

"Mr. Pierce, Lucas Leary is the alias we want you to forget!" Dr. Levy said insistently.

"Are you fucking with me Jasmine?" Lucas asked heatedly.

"No Mr. Pierce, you have been here for some time now under the mislaid belief that your name is Lucas Leary" Dr. Levy replied.

"Bullshit! I want to see my brother and sisters!" Lucas said in a raised voice.

"Mr. Pierce as far as we know you never had a brother or sisters. In fact, your friends Caleb, Vincent, Jacob, Joseph and Emily are ostensibly fabrications also" Dr. Levy said with a stern face.

"What the absolute fuck are you talking about? You drugged
me with LSD or something and forced me into a psychotic
break so you can spin me these mind games you fucking
bitch!" Lucas yelled.

"Mr. Pierce these people have been derived by you from
multiple sources to substantiate an impressive backstory you
invented for yourself. It's not real!" Dr. Levy impressed upon
Lucas.

"Let me the fuck out of this goddamn room now!" Lucas
said.

Dr. Levy suddenly changed her demeanor and peered over
the top of the table at Lucas with a big grin.

"Lucas, you're not leaving us anytime soon! You are our
property until I say so and any time you look like you're
getting better we'll be slipping you more potent psychedelics.
When we're done you won't know your ass from your
elbow" Dr. Levy laughed as she walked out of the room.

Lucas yelled obscenities that reverberated down the hall
behind Dr. Jasmine Levy. With no hope in sight of ever being
discharged from this psychiatric hellhole Lucas lay there
knowing he was up a certain creek without a paddle.

Lucas Leary was from here on out a P.O.W. of the system.

Patient Lucas Leary and prisoner Earl Pierce.